WHY THEY RUN THE WAY THEY DO

stories

SUSAN PERABO

Simon & Schuster
New York London Toronto Sydney New Delhi

Simon & Schuster
1230 Avenue of the Americas
New York, NY 10020

First Simon & Schuster hardcover edition February 2016

SIMON & SCHUSTER and colophon are registered trademarks of
Simon & Schuster, Inc.

For information about special discounts for bulk purchases,
please contact Simon & Schuster Special Sales at 1-866-506-1949
or business@simonandschuster.com.

The Simon & Schuster Speakers Bureau can bring authors to your
live event. For more information or to book an event, contact the
Simon & Schuster Speakers Bureau at 1-866-248-3049 or visit our
website at www.simonspeakers.com.

Interior design by Lewelin Polanco

Manufactured in the United States of America

10 9 8 7 6 5 4 3 2 1

Library of Congress Cataloging-in-Publication Data

Perabo, Susan, 1969–
   [Short stories. Selections]
   Why they run the way they do : stories / Susan Perabo.—First Simon &
Schuster hardcover edition.
      pages ; cm
   I. Title.
   PS3566.E673A6 2016
   813'.54—dc23
2015025570

ISBN 978-1-4767-6143-5
ISBN 978-1-4767-6145-9 (ebook)

for Brady and Chase
■■■ ■

CONTENTS

THE PAYOFF

When they gave us lumps of clay in art class, I made a pencil holder in the shape of a giraffe, and Louise made an ashtray. She molded and baked it, lopsided and heavy as a brick, as a birthday present for her mom, who smoked Kents vigorously and ground them flat with a callused thumb. So Louise had made this poop-brown ashtray, but she'd left it in the art room cooling outside the kiln and didn't remember it until after school, halfway through softball. When practice ended I yelled to my mom to wait on us and we ran back into the building—the side door was always open until five, so kids with softball and soccer could pee—and thundered down the stairs to the basement where the art room was. We didn't know if it would be unlocked or not, but we thought we'd give it a shot.

Louise reached the door first—it was one of those doors with nine little windows, to give kids nine separate chances at breaking something. No sooner had she put her hand on the knob and her face to the middle pane when she reeled back from the door like someone had grabbed a fistful of her long red hair and *yanked* her back.

"Bullshit," she said, for this was our favorite swear word, and we used it indiscriminately.

"What?" I, too, stepped to the window and was repelled back a step by what I saw inside: our principal, Dr. Dunn, was standing in the archway of the supply closet with his pants crumpled at his ankles and his hands clawing through the short black hair of Ms. McDaniel, our art teacher, who knelt in front of him with her mouth—well, I'd seen enough. I turned to Louise and we both stared at each other in horror and mute shock for what must have been ten full seconds. Then, at once, we both exploded into riotous laughter and burst into motion away from the scene of the crime, ran full blast down the hall and up the stairs, laughing and gasping for air. By the time we slid into the backseat of my mother's paneled station wagon we had our poker faces set, but the image of what we'd witnessed was so vivid in my mind I couldn't believe my mother couldn't see it herself, reflected with perfect detail in the pools of my eyes.

■■■ ■

I had two little brothers, Nick and Sam. Their lives revolved around farting, Indian burns, and the timeworn torture of repeating everything you said, repeating everything you said. Someday I would enjoy the company of them both, my mother assured me, but until then I would need to exercise tolerance.

"Time for Grade Your Day," my father said from behind the curtain of steam that rose from his baked potato. "Anne?"

Though research had not yet proven it, my parents were certain that a well-balanced dinner together and a thorough discussion of the day's events would make us confident and bright children. They didn't know it would actually raise our SAT scores, but they were on the right track.

"B," I said, forking a stalk of asparagus.

"D-minus-plus-minus-and-a-half," said Sam. He was six.

"A-triple plus!" exclaimed Nick.

My father raised his eyebrows. "Win the lottery?"

"Nuh-uh." Nick grinned. "Two fifth graders got in a fight. They were both named Ben, and one of 'ems tooth got knocked out and flew about fifty feet down the hall."

"How awful," my mother said.

"Did Ben start it?" my father asked, winking at me. Though I was only three years older than Nick, I got to be in on all my father's jokes. "How 'bout you, kiddo?" he asked me. "News of the day?"

"Mrs. Payne subbed in math."

"Oh no," my mother said. "I thought they'd finally gotten rid of her."

I shrugged. "She was there."

"Mrs. Payne is a pain in the butt," Nick said, and Sam snorted.

"That's original," I said. "Only every single person ever to go to our school for the last hundred years has said that."

"Learn anything?" my father asked, undeterred.

I had learned what a blowjob (or BJ, as Louise told me on the phone before dinner) looked like. I had learned that men didn't actually need to remove their underpants to have sex.

"I learned how to bunt," I said. "At practice."

"Just hold the bat out there," my father said, pretending his steak knife was a Louisville Slugger and wiggling it over his slab of meat. "Just let the ball hit the bat, right?"

"And keep your fingers out of the way," I added.

"That's the most important part," my mother agreed, for my mother was a dodger from way back. In supermarket aisles, she was always the one scooting her cart around to make room for everybody else.

■■■ ■

I was regarded with bemused suspicion in the Hanley home, because when Louise and I were in first grade my parents had voted for Richard Nixon. They'd staked a big red sign in our front yard—

4

MORE

YEARS!

—which is how the Hanleys even knew about it in the first place. Now, even with a Democrat in the White House (a peanut farmer, my father was forever pointing out, with a brother on *Hee Haw*) Mrs. Hanley still couldn't let it drop.

"There she is again," she would say wryly, smoke puffing from her nostrils. "President of the Young Republicans."

"Mom . . ." Louise would sigh. "Anne is not—"

"—anything," I would finish. "I'm not anything. I swear."

On the mantel, in the place where most people had photos of grinning offspring, Mr. and Mrs. Hanley had framed pictures of John and Bobby Kennedy, looking contemplative and doomed.

There was a Spiro Agnew Velcro dartboard on the refrigerator and a faded bumper sticker slapped crookedly across the oven window that said "50 Americans Died Today In Vietnam." The Hanleys got at least four different newspapers and apparently felt the need to keep them handy for quick reference; there were waist-high stacks of them in every room of the house except for Louise's bedroom. Mrs. Hanley always sat at the dining room table scouring the articles and smoking her Kents, and when Mr. Hanley came home from work he sat on a tattered lawn chair in the middle of the backyard with his feet soaking in a little yellow tub and read until dark.

My mother called them eccentric; she didn't like all the time I spent there, and she often pumped me to find out if Mrs. Hanley had said anything unusual or confusing, anything that had left me feeling *uneasy*. I never gave a thing away; I'd learned earlier than most that the less your parents knew about the concrete details of your day, the better off you were. My father thought the Hanleys were lunatics, but unlike my mother, he believed it was important for me to be exposed to lunatics—provided they were harmless—in order to be a well-rounded adult.

The day after we saw what we saw in the art room, Louise and I holed up after school in the Hanleys' basement. Ever since Louise's sister had left for college, we had the basement to ourselves: the paneled walls, the matted shag carpet, the stale air of twenty-thousand cigarettes smoked by unhappy members of the generation that directly preceded ours.

"Ms. McDaniel should watch out," Louise said. She was sucking on a Charms Blow Pop, twirling it back and forth over her tongue. "She could get a disease doing that."

Louise knew things. Her sister, Donna, was seven years older, a freshman in college, and willing to talk. Plus, the Hanleys let Louise see R-rated movies and read whatever books she wanted. I'd looked at *Playboy* at her house one time, right at the dining room table. My mother wouldn't even let me read *Seventeen* in checkout lines.

"What kind of disease?" I asked.

"You don't even want to know," Louise said, which was her answer when she herself didn't know. "I wonder if they do that every day."

"I bet they do other things, too," I said, and with no warning whatsoever a vivid picture flashed into my mind of Ms. McDaniel carefully painting Dr. Dunn's penis with the very same blue watercolors we'd used last week on our skyscapes. I blushed at my own fantasy: I hadn't even known I had the capacity to create such an image.

"Dr. Dunn," Louise said thoughtfully, tapping her Blow Pop on her top teeth. "Dr. Dickdunn. Dr. Dunn Dick Dunderhead."

"Remember last year," I said, "when he yelled at Melanie Moon when she dropped her Rube Goldberg project in the hallway and spilled all that corn oil?"

She scoffed. "He's such an asshole. We could get him in big trouble, you know. We could turn him in to the school board."

"Would he get fired?"

"Sure he would. Plus his wife would divorce him and his kids would hate him and he'd lose all his friends. And everywhere he went people would make sucking sounds."

She slurped obscenely on her Blow Pop and I laughed. On the wall behind her was a torn poster that said "What if they had a war and nobody came?" which I had never understood because if "they" had a war then at the very least "they" would be there, so it wasn't really accurate to say that *nobody* came.

"Hey," Louise said. "What about blackmail?"

I frowned. "What about it?"

"We could do blackmail on him. Say we'll turn him in unless he pays up."

"Pays *money*?"

"No, Anne—gum. Of course money. Jeez." She tossed her Blow Pop stick in a nearby ashtray.

"How much you think we could ask for?" I said.

"We should start small," she said, her eyes narrowing. "That's how you do it. You get 'em on the hook. You make 'em think it's just one time. Then you start to squeeze a little more, and a little more, and—"

I shook my head. "You're making this up. You don't know bull-shit."

"What's to know?" she asked. "It's easy money."

■■■　■

It was hard to look at Ms. McDaniel on Monday. Sitting at our art table—once a victim of the school cafeteria, now dying a slow death of scissor scars and clotted paste—Louise and I smirked at each other and in the general direction of the supply closet, but neither of us managed to look up to the front of the room for several minutes. We entirely missed the instructions for the day's project, so when everyone started climbing out of the table and filing out the door, we had no idea why and had to ask around. Turned out we were supposed to go outside and search for nature; this week's project was a spring collage.

Ms. McDaniel oversaw our progress from the front steps of the school, and I found my eyes passing over her again and again. I wondered exactly what it was that Dr. Dunn saw in her that led him down the sinful path to the art room. She was new this year and it showed; she always seemed apprehensive when she talked to us as a group, as if at any moment we might all stand up and start squirting glue at her. She loosened up once we started working, when she could meander around the room murmuring words of encouragement and gentle direction. She wore short skirts and had bobbed hair just under her ears, like she was a tomboy before she became a teacher. She didn't have much in the way of boobs, hardly more than Louise and me, and we weren't even wearing bras yet.

Louise nudged me. "Check that out," she said. I followed her gaze to the window of the principal's office, which faced the front lawn. Dr. Dunn was standing at the window with his arms crossed over his chest, looking out at us. We could only see him from the waist up, and for a moment I imagined he didn't have any pants on, that his penis was dangling just out of view. I shook the thought from my head.

"He's gross," Louise said. "He's practically licking his lips."

"Why do you think he likes her?"

"They always like young ones," Louise said. "Donna said she could pick any man out of a crowd and he'd have sex with her, whether he was married or a hundred years old."

"Not any man," I said, thinking of my father standing among the men in Donna's crowd, my father with his shaggy hair and laugh lines around his mouth. Then I imagined my brothers grown up, tall and bearded but making armpit farts in a frantic attempt to draw Donna's attention.

Louise shrugged. "Check this out," she said, handing me a piece of notebook paper. In wavy, capital letters was written:

Dear Dr. Dunn,

It has come to our attention that you are having sexual relations with the art teacher Laurie McDaniel. Do not ask how we have the information, we just do. Unless you want everyone to find out your secret, put twenty dollars in an envelope and leave it behind the toilet in the middle stall in the second floor girls bathroom. Do this tomorrow (Tuesday) or face the consequences.

—x and y

"Am I X or Y?" I asked, handing the letter back.

"You're Y," Louise said.

"How come?"

"Because I'm X."

"Y is stupid," I said. "Nobody ever heard of Y. How come we can't both be X?"

"Two X's," she said, rolling her eyes. "Uh-huh. That would look really cool, Anne, really professional."

"No, just one X," I said. "For both of us. Just because we're two people we don't have to be two letters."

"Girls!" Ms. McDaniel shouted. She was standing at the front door waving us in. Her hair was fluttering in the breeze and I recalled how it had moved in waves under Dr. Dunn's thick fingers.

———

■■■　■

On our way to math after lunch, two more floppy salmon swept along in the river of students, I shrewdly allowed Louise's letter to fall from my fingers and onto the floor outside the main office. The letter was folded and taped closed and said "DR DUNN" in big block letters we tore from the library copy of *Ranger Rick,* so we assumed the secretary would discover it and simply pass it along to him. I sat in math class imagining him at his giant desk, unfolding the letter, staring at it for a moment, then slowly folding it again. Perhaps after school he'd go down to the art room, wave it in Ms. McDaniel's face.

"They've got us right where they want us,"

he'd say, or:

"The jig's up."

Maybe she would kiss him, poke her tongue between his lips.

"Darling," she would whisper against his teeth. *"What will we do?"*

"We'll think of something . . ."

He'd fit his hands over her small breasts, rub them with his thumbs.

"Anne?"

I looked up at Mrs. Payne. She was standing at the blackboard in her hideous orange and white flowered dress, her stomach and breasts an indistinguishable flowery lump. Her grotesque bottom lip trembled slightly, and her words came layered in saliva: "Problem four?"

I didn't know anything about problem four. That was problem one. Problem two was that thinking about Dr. Dunn and Ms.

McDaniel together had made me feel like I had a bubble expanding in my stomach, emptying me of everything but its own strained vulnerability, filling me up with the most palpable absence I'd ever known. My face was numb below my cheekbones and I felt sad and happy at the same time.

"Problem four," Mrs. Payne croaked.

A word about Mrs. Payne. My mother (and countless others) had complained to Dr. Dunn about her on several occasions, for Mrs. Payne was prone to catastrophic mood swings of blinding speed. One minute she'd be the sweetest old lady you'd ever known, a cuddle and a peppermint at the ready, and the next she'd turn on you like a viper, call you lazy, stupid, hopeless, slobber insults on you until you cried or (in the now famous case of Chris Brewster) wet your pants. Other times she'd seem positively adrift; at least once in a day she began a sentence with "When Mr. Payne was alive . . ." and then would launch into a story that might or might not have anything to do with the subject at hand or even with Mr. Payne himself. For instance, we'd be talking about fractions and suddenly Mrs. Payne would say, "When Mr. Payne was alive, you could buy a sporty car for five-hundred dollars. I had such a car myself that I drove all the way from Moline, Illinois, to Boise, Idaho, to visit my dear cousin Edith who was so distraught over a man that the only word she'd spoken for a year was 'pecan.'"

She'd pause. To remember? To consider? Why "pecan"? And then she'd move on as if no interruption had occurred.

"Fourteen," Louise whispered from behind me. In addition to her numerous other afflictions, Mrs. Payne was also half-deaf, so it was pretty easy to cheat on her.

"Fourteen," I said. My lips were dry and I licked them.

"Fourteen," Mrs. Payne said, as if mulling over the existence of the number itself. "Fourteen. Four-tee-een. Fourteen is correct."

"Space case," Louise said as we gathered our books at the end of class. "Thinking about how to spend the money?"

"Yeah," I said.

■■■ ■

The payoff came as two ten-dollar bills, as perfectly crisp as the ones my grandmother always sent for my birthday. Louise and I hit the bathroom between second and third periods the next morning, when it was packed with primping sixth graders, so that if Dr. Dunn was casing the joint he wouldn't be able to tell who'd actually made the pickup. It was me who went into the middle stall, me who with trembling fingers opened the envelope, certain it would contain a note that said "Anne Foster you are expelled from school for the rest of your life." But no—there were the two stiff tens, Alexander Hamilton with his sly grin—and I slid the envelope into my backpack and remembered to flush the toilet for cover, even though I hadn't used it, and when I emerged from the stall I gave Louise the sign, which was to brush the side of my nose with my index finger. We had seen this in *The Sting*.

"What're you gonna get?" Louise asked. "Think your mom'll take us to the mall this weekend?"

We were in the Hanleys' basement again and I felt like I'd swallowed the twenty dollars—in pennies. My stomach seemed to be sagging to my thighs.

"What's wrong?" Louise asked.

"We're gonna get caught," I said. "We're gonna get caught and my parents are going to kill me."

She rolled her eyes. "They're not going to kill you. What's the worst thing they could do to you, legally?"

"They could be very disappointed," I said. In my mind I could clearly see my parents' Very Disappointed faces, the unique mixture of grief and ire and guilt and pity I was fairly sure the two of them had begun assembling the moment they'd met, so profound and effective it was.

"Tough life," Louise said. "World's smallest violin, Anne."

I had known for years that Louise envied what she perceived as my perfect life and family. What she didn't know was that sometimes—like today—I envied hers. Whenever I did something I knew was wrong I wished my parents would die in a tragic car accident ASAP, before the truth of my flawed character could be revealed. It was an extreme solution, but the only one I could conceive of. Lucky Louise . . . the news of her own flawed character would cause little disruption in the Hanley house. Her mother probably wouldn't even look up from the paper.

"We could get two records each," Louise said. "Or we could save it to spend at Six Flags this summer."

"What if we bought something for Ms. McDaniel?"

She stared at me. "What?"

"I don't know." I dug my hands into the shag carpet. "Just, you know. We could buy her something. You know, with part of it."

She shook her head slowly. "You're a freak, Anne. Do you know that?"

"So?" I said. "You're a freak too."

"But you're a different kind of freak than me," she said thoughtfully. She twisted some hair around her finger. "I come from freaks. But you, like, sprouted up all on your own."

"So?"

"So fine," she said. "I'm just making an observation. What d'ya want to buy her, ya freak? Frilly underwear?"

"No," I said, my cheeks warming. "Something cool. Like, drawing pencils or something."

"Drawing pencils," she said flatly. "You've thought about this."

I shrugged.

She gazed at me impatiently, with the look of someone who in two or three years would no longer want to be my friend. We were two weird kids who had leapt from the ship of fools and splashed blindly toward each other, scrambled aboard the same life raft. Perhaps it was only a matter of time before we leapt again and made for separate shores.

She threw me one of the tens. "It's your money," she said.

■■■ ■

The next day I ditched recess after lunch and ran with a full heart to the art room. Ms. McDaniel was sitting at her desk nibbling on celery sticks and reading a thick book that bore no title on its cover. I shifted from one foot to the other in the doorway until she noticed me.

"Hello, Anne," she said, sliding the book into a desk drawer. She cocked her head cheerfully in the way of young teachers and enthusiastic babysitters. "What can I do for you?"

"I found these," I said. I approached her desk with the pencils held at arm's length in front of me. "Yesterday my mom needed to go to Art Mart and she gave me five dollars to spend and the thing that I wanted cost three-fifty so I picked these up off the sale table that was right next to the cash register and I thought you might want them."

Exhausted from the lie—I'd practiced it a dozen times that morning in the shower—I dropped the pencils on the desk beside her lunch bag. She looked at them curiously, then at me.

"Well, thank you," she said. "That's quite a story."

"It's what happened," I said emphatically, thinking she was on to my lie, but shortly thereafter realizing she was merely making conversation.

"You're very thoughtful," she said. She brushed a wayward hair from her forehead. "I love working with pencils."

"I know," I said. "One time you said that. In class, I mean. You mentioned that."

"I don't think I realized you had such an interest in art," she said.

"Sure," I said. I looked at her as she smiled expectantly, and I wanted to tell her that she didn't have to do all those things to Dr. Dunn, even if he was the principal. "Art's good," I said. "It's, you know, it's really . . . it's amazing."

"What did you get at Art Mart?" she asked.

"Paper," I said.

"Drawing paper?"

"Yes," I said. "White."

"Well, it's very thoughtful of you to think of me," she said again. She wadded up her brown paper bag and turned to throw it in the trash can, and when she did, the collar of her shirt shifted so that I could see her bra strap. In a burst of vivid color I imagined Dr. Dunn sinking his teeth into that shoulder, tugging on that bra strap like a dog with a rope, and I felt so dizzy I had to hold on to the desk to keep from falling over.

"Anne?" Ms. McDaniel said, turning back to me. "Honey, are you okay?"

Dear Dr. Dunn,

If you want to keep your affair quiet, place forty dollars in the envelope and put it in the appointed place.

The x's

ps Don't you think you're a little old for Ms. McDaniel?

Louise frowned. "What the hell is this?"

We were sitting on the school bus in our usual seat, fourth from the back on the right. This particular bus, for reasons none of us understood, always smelled like tuna salad in the morning and Bit-O-Honey in the afternoon.

"What's wrong with it?" I asked.

She ripped the paper in two and dropped it in my lap. "This is about blackmail," she said. "This is not about you being the pope or something."

"She's nice," I said. The bus went in and out of a pothole and the boys in the back seats whooped. "He's just using her for sex."

"Anne," she said. "You don't know anything about this. You don't have any idea what it's like to be an adult."

"Neither do you," I said, though I was realizing more and more this wasn't really true.

"I'm the letter writer from now on," she said. "We're just gonna stick to blackmail. We're not going to get into stuff we don't know anything about."

■■■ ■

We dropped off the note the next morning, with directions that forty dollars be left in the usual spot by sixth period. Right after lunch, Louise went to the nurse's office and—according to another kid who was there with a splinter in his palm—barfed the Thursday Special (Sloppy Joe, Tater Tots) in a steaming pile at Nurse Carol's feet. So Louise got sent home to the loving arms of her mother, and I was left alone to secure the afternoon's payoff.

We had planned poorly; my sixth period class was in the west wing of the building, three halls and a flight of stairs away from the bathroom in question. By the time I reached it the warning bell for seventh period had already rung. A couple girls were drying their hands and rushing out when I bolted myself into the middle stall and reached behind the toilet. Despite my tardiness (the final bell was sounding as I grasped my prize), I remained in the stall and tore open the envelope. Inside was a 3 x 5 notecard on which was printed, in tidy black letters:

Anne, Louise: There is nothing to tell. This foolishness ends right now.

Something that felt like cold water rushed from behind my ears all the way down to my heels. My brain flailed about sense-lessly for at least ten seconds before lighting upon the first thing it could recognize—*I have to get to social studies*. Hands trembling, I started at the latch, then froze when I heard the door to the hallway *whoosh* open. Six footsteps on soft-soled shoes, then silence.

"Louise?" I whispered hopefully, though I knew full well that Louise was at home safe in bed, which is exactly where I wished I were.

"It's not Louise."

It was Ms. McDaniel. I stood in the stall, my knees quaking, wondering: If I didn't open the door, didn't come out willingly, how long would she stand there? An hour? Overnight? Until school let out for the summer? I imagined my family sitting around the dinner table waiting for me, years passing, my mother's patience waning, my father's smile turning melancholy, my brothers stealing away with their own Ms. McDaniels.

I slid the latch to the side, let the door swing open of its own accord. She was leaning against the wall next to the paper-towel dispenser. Her face was all blotchy and her lips were somehow crooked, but she wasn't crying. She looked like she should be in the emergency room.

"Well?" she said.

"Hi," I said.

I was standing there holding the index card; I could have run but it seemed pointless. Suddenly she sprang from the wall and grabbed my wrist, twisted it until the note dropped to the floor. Still gripping my wrist, she leaned over and picked it up, read it once, then read it again. Then she straightened up, loosened her grasp, and regarded me coolly.

"Are you satisfied?" she asked.

I had no idea what she meant. More important, I didn't know which answer would get me out the door faster. "Yes," I said, then changed my mind. "I mean no. Yes and no. Not really. Sort of." I bit my lip.

"Someday you'll know what it's like to really love someone," she said. She said it kind of gently, like she was talking to a little kid. "Some day you'll know what it's like to look at a man, his neck and his knees and his warm hands, and know that everything that was missing in your life has come knocking."

"Ms. McDaniel—" I said. I'm not sure what I had it in my mind to say, but it didn't really matter, because she wasn't listening.

"And someday, Anne Foster," she said. "Someday some awful little girl you don't even know will ruin your life for no reason. And when that day comes I want you to think of me."

■■■ ■

Louise called that night and my father came to get me. I buried my head in my math book and told him I had to study for a test tomorrow. When she called again I told him the same thing. He returned to my room a few minutes later.

"Louise says you don't have a test in math tomorrow."

"She wouldn't know," I said. "She had to go home early today."

He leaned in the doorway. "Everything okay?"

I wanted to tell him what had happened in the bathroom. I wanted him to sit on the edge of my bed and explain point for point what had transpired, help me understand what Ms. McDaniel had said to me. But I knew, somehow more than I'd ever known anything, that even had I the courage to ask the questions (which I did not) that he would be unable to answer a single one of them. It was a realization that left me cold: the machinations of the human heart were inexplicable, not only to me, but to my parents as well, and thus, apparently, to anyone. Was this what Louise had known all along? I wondered. Was there truly no one in her life from whom she had ever, *ever*, expected a satisfying explanation?

"Everything's fine," I said.

■■■ ■

"You're gonna have to tell me sometime," Louise said from her seat at the desk behind me. We were in math class.

I turned to her, deliberately put my finger to my lips.

"What the hell?" she said. "What happened to you?"

"When Mr. Payne was alive . . ." Mrs. Payne began.

Mrs. Payne, a pain in the butt, a punch line to the joke of every fifth grader. Yesterday she'd been as flat and clear as a pane of glass. Today I gazed through her sagging breasts and jowls and saw her as a young woman, as young as Ms. McDaniel, a mystery slipping out of her nightgown and into the arms of her beloved.

MICHAEL THE ARMADILLO

They'd made it through all the Michaels, Carrie and Dan believed, made it through Michael Jordan and Michael Douglas and Michael Moore and Michael J. Fox, made it through the terrible summer when Michael Phelps won all those gold medals in swimming, and then the next terrible summer when Michael Jackson died on every channel for days and days, dodged a bullet when Michaels, the crafts store, canceled plans to open in their town (that would have been hell—Dan drove by that strip mall every day on his way to work). Once at a library program when Chloe was two they'd been forced to sing "Michael Row the Boat Ashore," but Dan was in the bathroom and missed the whole sordid tune, and by the time he returned everyone was mechanically rolling their fists around to "Wheels on the Bus." They had survived the Michaels, hadn't bumped into a big, noisy one for over a year, seemed to have found their most solid footing, and when the occasional Michael was mentioned on television, or when their waiter at Chili's wore the vulgar name on his name tag, their world did not lurch to an awkward halt and the piece of them that had already perished a thousand times did not perish again. They, Carrie and Dan both, had pulled through. It had taken six years and one baby girl but they'd made it, together, they'd weathered the storm of Michael, and they were going to be okay.

And then out of the blue one day late in February—no birthday or holiday in sight, no earthly reason—Dan's mother sent Chloe a package with a stuffed armadillo puppet inside and Chloe snatched the animal from the box and hugged it and exclaimed: "Michael! Michael!"

It was early evening, the best time of the day, the sudden, painless shedding of work and preschool complete, the familiar comfort of worn couch cushions and the temperamental garbage disposal. They were in the kitchen, Chloe and Dan at the table (Chloe kneeling on the chair) and Carrie standing at the stove, stirring something in a pot—she couldn't have said what it was in that moment, not if someone had had a knife to her throat.

"How do you know that's his name?" Dan asked, in the most nonchalant tone he could muster.

"Michael! It's Michael!" Chloe said, joyfully, bouncing on her knees. She stuffed her hand into the hole in the armadillo's belly, wiggled her fingers into its head, then thrust it toward her father's face. "I'm Michael," she said, in her armadillo voice, which was her voice for every animal, a low monotone with a hint of a speech impediment.

"Is he on TV?" asked Carrie from the stove, a panicky, hopeful lilt to her voice, as if she were calling up the stairs in an empty house. Dan looked briefly in her direction, but his eyes were not able to land on his wife. His glance began darting uncontrollably around the room, fly-like. It had been years since this had happened and he was furious and humiliated to find it happening to him now, in front of his daughter, as if she'd notice, as if anyone but him had any idea.

Dan looked at his shoes. This was the only thing that helped.

"What d'ya mean, TV?" Chloe asked. She tried to spin the armadillo around on her finger and it flew off her hand and skittered across the floor to Carrie's feet. Chloe leapt up to retrieve it.

"Does he have a TV show?" Dan asked, looking up, his eyes back under his own power. "Have you seen him on some—"

"No," Chloe said, smacking a kiss on her mother's knee with the fuzzy, twisted mouth of the puppet. "He's just here, in our house. He's mine. He's—"

■■■ ■

—*goddamn Michael the goddamn armadillo,* Carrie thought, standing in the backyard, smoking her cigarette. An armadillo! Really? What a stupid animal! Who sent a child an armadillo? Who would even *make* a stuffed armadillo, ugly and scuttling, awkwardly prehistoric? She took a deep drag and let it out as slowly as she could. She allowed herself one cigarette in the backyard every night, after Chloe was asleep and Dan was watching TV or doing the dishes. She also allowed herself to eat a small Baggie of gummie bears before lunch, at her desk. She allowed herself to sleep late on Sundays. She allowed herself to be ten minutes late for work, as long as she was thinking about work (and thus, more or less, working) during the ten-minute drive to her office. She allowed herself to buy the expensive toilet paper. She allowed herself to take showers that were environmentally irresponsible. She allowed herself to think about Michael, but only when she was stopped at a train crossing and alone (completely alone—not even Chloe) in the car, and then the *ca-clack ca-clack ca-clack* was her permission to disengage from her current situation—her family, her home, her *life*—and when the train had passed and her car was bumping over the tracks she stopped thinking about him and allowed herself to go on with her day.

She'd been with Michael six years before, very briefly—one week at a professional workshop in Boston. It had been a whirlwind: three days of friendship, two days of courting, then two frantic, ecstatic days in her room when she felt so unlike herself, so shameless and reckless, so joyfully unguarded, that in moments she wondered if she were dreaming or dead. She told herself on the Sunday morning before they parted, as they lay tangled in bed, *You will tell yourself that you did not feel like this. You will tell yourself that it wasn't extraordinary, but you will be lying in order to not torture yourself. You will tell yourself this didn't mean anything, but that will not be true.* It was a terrible thing, what she did to herself that day. In that tangled moment she pretended it was a gift she was giving to her future self, but really it was pure cruelty—cold-blooded, premeditated murder—because she knew her own weaknesses, and she chose to exploit them, and she knew she would cripple her future self with doubt and misery, possibly for the rest of her life. And yet she—this present Carrie—had thwarted that cruel self, that old murderer. It had taken some time, but ultimately she had triumphed, limiting that self, that curse, to the *ca-clack ca-clack ca-clack* of the swiftly passing train, and she really did not think about Michael, or that vicious trick she'd played on herself, at any other time, not anymore. It was another life, six years that seemed like sixty, a life before

Chloe, before she'd figured out what was important, what she really wanted. It was a stupid mistake, a moment of recklessness. It was not who she was.

■■■ ■

And yet she had written to him for seven months after that weekend in Boston. Dan knew this. Dan knew *everything*. He had made it his business to find out everything, after she had admitted to it. She'd told him one morning in their bedroom, while they were getting dressed for work. He never knew what it was that finally compelled her to spill it, but when she spilled it she *spilled* it, nearly vomiting out the truth, standing there in her underwear beside the closet, trembling, weeping the ugliest tears he'd ever seen. She'd never kept a secret in their seven years of marriage, maybe not ever in her life, and watching it wrest out of her was like witnessing an exorcism. She said, she blubbered: "I know you'll want to leave me. I'll understand." And then, the filthy cat out of the foul bag, she had gone to work, with no makeup and wet hair, and wearing two different shoes (he noticed this when he looked out the bedroom window and watched her get into the car), and then he went through the house like a goddamn DEA agent, ripping clothes off hangers, digging into every coat pocket, emptying entire desk drawers onto the floor. He would have slit open the couch cushions if he hadn't suddenly looked at the computer sitting there impassively on the desk in the living room and sat down and typed what—in a moment of desperate inspiration—he absolutely *knew* was her email password (though he'd never asked), the name of her childhood cat, and there was *everything*, in a tiny little mailbox icon marked ETC—ETC!—not only the other man's emails to her but, more damning and far more excruciating, hers to him.

But Dan, broken as he was, did not leave. By going to work Carrie had given him a window, a bay window, of several hours to gather his thoughts. The house was ransacked by 9:30, the emails read by 10:15, reread by 10:35, re-reread by 10:50. He'd called in sick (because you couldn't call in *shit on*) to work and there was a whole day ahead of him, brimming with endless possibility. He could pack his bags and leave, yes. He could be three states away—in any direction! he could go wherever he wanted!—by the time she pulled into the driveway. This was the first day of the rest of his life. He was not so old—only twenty-nine. He could begin again, reinvent himself. "I'll understand," she had said. But she had conspicuously not said "I'm leaving," not said "the marriage is over." She had left the choice to him. She had probably thought he would leave her, probably wanted him to leave her, probably was sitting at her desk pricing flights to Phoenix (this is where the man lived, he'd learned from the emails), preparing for the big, romantic reunion with Michael the tax accountant who had rocked her world in Boston. In the letters there had been phrases like "When we're finally together" and "I can't wait until we . . ." as if it were only a matter of time. But Carrie had not left him this morning, had not said she was leaving him, had instead, importantly, crucially, said, "I know you'll want to leave me." And now she was at work, fully expecting him to be here packing his things, using this bay window of time to get his affairs in order, to box up the marriage in her absence so she could be free (she used this word in one of the letters: "free") to go to Phoenix and join Michael the tax accountant who had rocked her world in Boston. She was leaving the ball in his court, lobbing up a big fat fattie across the net, like she used to do when they'd played in college, so he could have his overhead slam and feel like a big man, but guess what? *Fuck her!* He said this aloud, at 11:13, standing among their lives dumped out on the floor. *Fuck her!* He'd show her, all right. No way was he going to leave her! He hated her, so he wasn't going to leave her. And he loved her, so he wasn't going to leave her. She wanted him to do the dirty work, make it easy for her, open the door to her new life? Ha!

He cleaned the house. He didn't only clean *up* the house, he *cleaned* the house, first tidying his own frenzied mess and then vacuuming and dusting and scrubbing until his fingers ached so much that he couldn't make his hands into fists. He defrosted the freezer, tightened the rickety porch railing, changed the lightbulb in the garage that had been dark for two years. He showered and shaved and went to the grocery store and bought two slabs of tenderloin and baked potatoes and fresh corn on the cob. He made dinner and set the table and lit the candles and when she walked in the front door he put his arms around her and said, "We're going to be okay."

"We are?" she asked.

Now, six years later, Dan stood in his daughter's room, watching her sleep. She had saved them, softened his rage, centered Carrie's world. And it wasn't just that they loved her—of course they loved her, madly—but rather that their love for each other was altered, irrevocably, by her squirming body, lifted from Carrie's belly (he'd seen *inside* his wife, seen the startled eyes of his daughter looking up from her mother's womb) and set stickily and miraculously into his trembling hands.

Chloe was clutching the armadillo, but she slept soundly so it was easy to slide it from her arms and insert, in its place, a red rabbit with a star for a nose. He knew that Chloe had little attachment to individual animals. She had never had the best-loved-bear, no tattered dog she mourned if it were left behind—he'd heard such stories from other dads. They were mostly interchangeable to her, these animals, and she had, it seemed, hundreds of them, all of which she loved for a day or two until another in the room caught her eye. So he put the armadillo on a crowded shelf with another twenty once-loved animals and she rolled over onto the star-nosed rabbit and he went down the hall to his bedroom and his sleeping wife.

■■■ ■

In the morning Chloe came into the kitchen with the armadillo balanced on her head. Carrie was packing the lunchbox for preschool and her stomach dropped at the sight of the animal, whom she had seen first thing that morning, tucked on a shelf, only a fraction of it visible, when she'd crept into Chloe's room to do the same and found the deed already done.

"Look what Michael can do!" Chloe said.

Dan set down his coffee. "Where'd you get that?" he asked.

"Nana sent him," she said, spinning in circles.

"I know," he said. "I mean . . ."

Chloe stopped spinning. "Can I take Michael to school?"

"No," Carrie said, narrowly missing severing her entire thumb while slicing a pear. Or maybe that would be preferable, she thought. Things would have to be done, ambulances called, digits reattached, bloody counters scoured. No one would think about an armadillo.

"How come?"

Carrie shook her head. "You don't take toys to school."

"Sometimes I do," Chloe said. She scooched out her chair and sat down in front of her Cheerios, the armadillo still perched on her head. "For show and tell."

"Not today, honey," Carrie said.

"But—"

"Chloe, the answer is—"

"If she wants to take him to school, let her take him to school," Dan interrupted. "It's her armadillo."

"Yay!" Chloe said.

Carrie ran her tongue over her teeth. She'd just be quiet; that was best.

Dan solemnly crossed his arms and addressed the puppet on his daughter's head. "Now, Michael," he said. "This is a very serious matter. I have to ask you: Do you want to be in show and tell?"

"He does!" Chloe shouted.

"It's not for the faint of heart, Michael," Dan said. "Everyone will be looking at you. You'll be on display for all to see. Are you prepared for that, Michael?"

"Daddy, he wants to!"

"Do you understand what we're asking of you, Michael?"

Okay, then, Carrie thought, pitching Baggies into her daughter's lunch box. *All right, then.* This was how it was going to be. This was how he had chosen to play it. Okay. Accept. Accept and adjust. This was the price. This was the price you paid. Once, during the months of letters, she had written his name all over her body with a big red marker. She'd done it on her lunch hour, at work, in a bathroom stall, breathlessly, the tip of the pen like the tip of a finger. She had walked around for an entire day with him under her clothes, his name in thick letters on her stomach, her upper arms, her thighs.

She lay in bed with the word still there, her heart pounding, knowing if Dan turned to her and started something that all might be revealed. She'd been out of her mind, sick with desire. This was the price you paid for something like that.

When she'd come home that day, that terrible day, and found dinner on the table, the house clean, Dan still there, she realized her subconscious plan had gone awry. If only her plan had been just a little less *sub* she would have surely seen the obvious holes, been able to play out the possible scenarios. She had thought Dan would leave—that was why (subconsciously why, of course) she'd told him the truth—and now he hadn't left, apparently had no intention of leaving, and now her conscious self was left with the mess made by the subconscious. What was she supposed to do now? "We're going to be okay," he'd told her. "You're going to break that thing (thing!) off, and we're going to change and be better and happier and stronger people and we belong together and I'm not going anywhere."

Now she would have to leave him. She had to do it. It was the only thing to do. That night she lay in bed beside him. *I'll do it tomorrow,* she told herself. *Tonight of course I could not do it because he cleaned the house and made me dinner but I love someone else and that's not fair to anyone and so tomorrow I'll leave.* The next night she lay in bed, thinking how much she liked her bed, how much she liked her bed*room*, actually, how much she would miss it, this room, which she and Dan had painted together because they were too cheap to hire a painter and so there were paint smudges on the ceiling, permanent evidence of their mutual sloppiness. The next night she lay in bed, thinking of how many books they had and how it would be hell, dividing up all those books, how they'd have to sit down for hours, days even, side by side going through everything:

Was this his *One Hundred Years of Solitude* or hers? They'd taken The Contemporary Novel together in college and would have to look through the notes in the book and then they'd both remember what it had been like, sitting beside each other in that sunny classroom with the big windows, twenty years old, none the wiser. The next day the man in Phoenix sent her an email to which she did not respond. Two days later he sent her one that she deleted without reading. The next day he sent another, with a subject line that read:

?

■■■　■

On Saturday one of Chloe's preschool friends had a birthday party at Chuck E. Cheese. Chloe, with Michael the armadillo tucked under her arm, galloped into the restaurant with the other children and the attending parents. Carrie and Dan sat in the car in silence, until Carrie said:

"Promise me we'll never have a party at Chuck E. Cheese."

"I promise," Dan said. He fake-grimaced. "I hate that mouse."

"He's creepy," Carrie agreed. "More like a rat than a mouse."

"So what d'ya wanna do?" he asked. Drop-off parties were a relatively new thing in their lives. Dan couldn't think, now, what they would have done on a Saturday afternoon by themselves, before Chloe. How empty it must have been!—though they would not have known it, with nothing to compare it to.

"We could go have lunch somewhere . . . ?" she offered.

"We could do that," he said. "People do that."

When they returned to the restaurant an hour and a half later all the children were in a state of anxious fascination because one of the boys had tumbled out of a plastic tube and was bleeding from the mouth. The birthday girl's parents, mortified that blood had been spilled on their watch, rushed everyone out of the restaurant so the injured boy could be tended to without an audience of gaping kids and judging parents. Halfway home Dan realized that the armadillo was not with them, had been left behind in their whirlwind departure. A few minutes later he saw Carrie realize it; she turned suddenly to the backseat and then to him, started to say something but stopped, looked again to the backseat, pretending to stretch. Chloe had fallen asleep, slumped awkwardly against her flowery restraints. When they arrived home Dan carried her into the house and lay her on the couch in the family room. When she woke later they all played HiHo! Cherry-O and watched *The Little Mermaid* and then she went to bed, still groggy from the festivities, still unaware of her loss.

■■■ ■

"Michael!"

Dan sat bolt upright in bed, heart pounding. A dream?

"Where's Michael?"

No. It was Chloe. Carrie stirred beside him as he swung out of bed.

"Daddy?" Chloe called as he neared her room, and he was happy it was him she wanted, his name on her lips, not Michael, not Mommy.

"It's okay, sweetie," he said. He sat down gently on the side of her bed and put his hand on her cheek. "You're okay."

"I can't find Michael," she said.

"Did you have him when you left the party?"

"I did," she said. Her eyes narrowed. "I *think* I did."

"Maybe you left him at Chuck E. Cheese."

She opened and closed her mouth slowly, always the preface to tears. "He's lost forever," she said.

He was aware that Carrie was behind him, in the doorway.

"You'll be okay, sweetie," he said. "Daddy's here."

"Maybe we can find another armadillo, honey," Carrie said softly.

"I don't want another armadillo!" Chloe shouted. "I only want Michael!"

But it wasn't true, not really. The next day, Sunday, without Carrie and Dan even having to discuss it, without a word to confirm they were on the same page, they went to Toys R Us and told Chloe she could pick out any animal she wanted. *Any* animal. She needed only a moment to decide, choosing a giant giraffe, as tall as Carrie, with leather hooves and ears. Dan got winded carrying it to the car. It was the kind of thing, Dan thought, that a movie star would buy for his daughter, or that a child battling cancer would receive from a charitable organization, one of those toys that a *regular* child would never get. On the way home Chloe covered its head with kisses and said, "You're my best friend ever."

That night they were in the kitchen eating ice cream when the phone rang. Dan picked up.

"Are you missing an armadillo?" the voice on the phone asked.

"I'm sorry?" Dan said.

"This is Lindsay's mom." Pause. "Lindsay. The birthday girl."

He didn't say anything.

"Lindsay, from preschool. You know, the birthday party. We

found an armadillo when we were cleaning up and Lindsay thought it was Chloe's."

Dan looked at the kitchen table, where the giraffe stood resolutely—like a tower, really, a pillar of strength, even—between his wife and daughter. A giraffe! Now there was an animal you could get behind. A giraffe was, well, Christ, let's face it, pretty remarkably goddamn seriously unbelievable. Eating leaves off the top of trees? Are you kidding me?

Chloe lifted her spoon of cookies-and-cream toward the giraffe's smiling mouth.

"Hello?" said the voice on the phone.

"It's not ours," Dan said. "It must belong to someone else."

■■■ ■

The next day at preschool pickup Chloe burst out the door of the four-year-old room waving the armadillo. "Look what Lindsay found!" she shouted. "I left him at Chuck E. Cheese!" She jammed the puppet into Carrie's stomach and began struggling into her puffy coat.

"Oh my," Carrie said. She turned the puppet over in her hands. Its eyes were black beads and they glinted in the bright lights of the preschool hallway. "Wow. Look at that."

"Is that yours?" Lindsay's mother asked, extracting herself from the clot of waiting parents.

"Ours?" Carrie asked. She was aware of herself blinking too many times—her eyes felt like black beads, too—as she looked at Lindsay's mother. She didn't even know the woman's name. Jane? Melissa? "Is it ours? It is ours, yes." She nodded. "Yes, it is."

"Mommy," Chloe said.

"Well, Lindsay thought so," the mother said, relieved. "But when we called last night your husband said it wasn't, so we thought we'd bring it in today and check with some of the other kids. I guess I should have asked you. My husband would have probably thought the same thing—can't tell one toy from another, can they?"

"It's hard for them to keep track," Carrie said softly, remembering Dan on the phone. "Wrong number!" he'd said, cheerfully.

"Mommy?" Chloe said.

"There's so much," Carrie said. "So many things . . ."

Lindsay's mom scoffed. "Like they even try!" She rolled her eyes conspiratorially, as if she and Carrie had an understanding, shared a history. As if she and her idiot husband were made of precisely the same cloth as Carrie and Dan.

"Dan's not like that," Carrie said. "He tries. He—"

"Now, Mommy!" Chloe exclaimed. Carrie looked down at her daughter, who had both hands clasped between her legs. "Right now!" she said.

■■■ ■

"Lindsay's having a baby," Chloe said at dinner. They all sat at the kitchen table, Chloe flanked by the giraffe—towering—and by the armadillo on the chair beside her, propped up on its tail and resting its paws on the table.

"I doubt that very much," Dan said.

"She is! In the summer."

"Maybe her mommy's having a baby," Carrie said.

"But Lindsay *gets* it," Chloe said.

"Sure," Carrie said. "Okay. I see what you're saying."

"Can I have a baby?" Chloe asked.

Carrie looked at Dan. They had talked about it before, of course. It had always seemed something they would do, when the time felt right. But years had passed quickly—how could Chloe already be almost five?—and they were so busy, both working. It could be a good thing, though. Four. For a while three had seemed right. They'd gotten used to three. They'd gotten used to a lot. But four. Four wasn't that many. She could give up her cigarette.

"Someday," she said.

"When?" Chloe asked.

"Sooner rather than later," Carrie said.

"Saturday?" Chloe asked.

Dan smiled. "Not quite that soon," he said.

■■■ ■

That night, after they put Chloe to bed, Dan sat down in the living room in front of a basketball game while Carrie went outside for her cigarette. He flipped through the paper, read all the bad news, waited for her to return. He wanted her to sit next to him on the couch, wanted to laugh at something on TV—some idiotic commercial, some know-it-all sportscaster, something that could draw them together, remind them that, in the little ways—and weren't those the ways that mattered, anyway?—they were on *the same page*. He craned his neck to see out the front window, thinking he might spot the glow from her cigarette, breathing as she breathed, but the yard was dark. Sometimes she went for a short walk, if the weather was nice, but it was cold outside and he couldn't imagine she would have gone far. At halftime he climbed the stairs and went into Chloe's room. The giraffe lay stiffly beside her, filling a good two-thirds of the bed, its leather hooves overshooting the mattress by six inches. The armadillo was out of sight—under Chloe, he imagined—but when he rolled her warm torso over to peek, he found nothing. He surveyed her room then, still no Michael, went down to the kitchen, walked through the living room, checking all the usual spots, under the couch, behind the chair pillows, inside the DVD cabinet. No armadillo. He went back upstairs, put on his pajamas, and brushed his teeth. He slipped into Chloe's room and looked out her window and down the street. His wife had been gone for almost an hour. A lot could happen in an hour.

But then he heard the front door open and close. She ascended the stairs, quietly, then tiptoed past Chloe's room and into their dark bedroom, the smell of cigarettes trailing in her wake. He followed her and stood in the doorway, a hand on either side of the doorframe, as if an earthquake were approaching. She was in the bathroom and he listened to the usual sounds of preparing for bed. When she opened the door she gasped to find him standing there, his shadow thrown into the dark room by the nightlight behind him in the hall.

"What did you do with it?" he asked.

"Jesus," she said. "You scared me." She walked over to the bed and set her alarm for morning. When he didn't move from his spot, she looked up at him. "You're very ominous, looming there in the doorway like that."

"What did you do with it?"

"With what?"

"You know with what."

"It's gone," she said, swinging her legs under the covers. "Just . . . it's gone."

He shook his head. "She's gonna cry."

"Maybe for a day. But then she'll be fine."

"Where'd you put it?"

She sighed. It was a sigh with a message. "Dan, he's gone, okay?"

"But where *is* he?"

She turned onto her stomach, slid her arms under her pillow. "He's nowhere," she said.

Nowhere? He gripped the doorframe tighter. Where was nowhere? Had she buried him at a construction site, tied a brick to his tail and thrown him in the river? Maybe she had cut him up into a million little pieces. He'd seen a movie once about a man escaping from jail, a prisoner who dug a tunnel from his cell with crude tools, and every morning the prisoner covered up the hole with a poster and put the rubble from the night's work into his pants pockets and went out into the yard and gently shook the rubble, crumb by crumb, from the holes he'd cut in the tips of his pants pockets and out the bottom of his pants legs, leaving it scattered across the jail yard, pebbles among pebbles, dust among dust, so no one was the wiser.

He looked at her lying there. She was pretending to sleep, but he knew she wasn't really. He was no fool. She wanted to skip this conversation, wanted to wake up in the morning with the issue too many hours closed to continue. He would not let her win. He would just stand here, his shadow covering her. He would stand here in this doorway until she was forced to say something more.

But as her breathing evened—could she really fake him out, after all these years?—the bed began to look more and more appealing.

He was tired. And he liked the bed, liked this whole bedroom, really, which he and Carrie had painted together years before because they were too cheap to hire a painter and so there were paint smudges on the ceiling. He went and sat on the edge of the bed, his back to her. Tomorrow was Tuesday. Tuesdays were always crazy; he needed a good night's sleep. He lay down and turned toward her, looked over her rising back and out the window. It was snowing. The snow was billowy; instead of falling it lifted and spun and sailed outward into the black sky. Watching the flakes whirl by the glass he imagined tiny, indistinguishable bits of Michael the armadillo, tiny puffs of fluff and pieces of brown fur, spinning from Carrie's pockets as she went throughout her day, covering the house, the yard, the world, so that instead of being gone, instead of being nowhere, he was everywhere.

STORY GOES

It's true that some things I did not witness first hand: the music therapist's half nelson; the chair with the built-in straps; the suitcases packed for college; the field. But I am a reliable witness to most of what happened that day. Certainly I can be sure of my role, which officially consisted of a paint-by-number and a Styrofoam cup of cranapple juice. About other, earlier days I am equally certain. About the woman who believed we were angels. About the phones that didn't ring. About the macramé noose. About the threads of drool that spooled from her lips after ECT. My memory is sharp. I keep it sharp. Ten smooth strokes a day on the sharpening stone, always in the same direction.

Madeline was four years older than me. She had long dark hair that hung in violent tangles. She was so skinny that I could have bench pressed her, despite my own weakened condition. She had been everywhere. She could have written a travel guide to hospitals across Missouri and Illinois: what to bring, how to dress, what foods to avoid, currency, language, customs. She had seen it all, seen people *raw*. She told me stories about the places she'd been and the things she had seen people do to themselves and to each other. She was nineteen and her life was almost over. She was in the home stretch.

About Simon & Garfunkel. About where we hid the screws. About the drinking fountain with the masking tape. About the bus. About the buffer boys. About morning stretch with the cripples. About the stuffed bunny in the clothes dryer. About croquet with foam mallets and rubber wickets.

"I need you to do something for me," she said. It was midmorning and we were supposed to be changing out of our scrubs but instead we were sitting on the heater in her room because it was the only really warm place in the whole unit and we were always cold. "I need your help."

She needed my help. *My* help. I couldn't remember the last time I had helped someone. My blood was so thick with prescription drugs that I could hardly hold a conversation. My eyes were dirty windshields, the whole world covered in a milky gray film. A year before I'd played junior varsity softball, ripped line drives up the middle. What had it been like to see the ball, not just the ball but its twirling seams, as it connected with my sparkling bat? I could not begin to recall this image, this sensation, nor even the girl in the batter's box who had felt it. I had only a vague sense that she had once existed, not a memory of her but a recollection of her presence, like the grandmother who dies when you are three.

"When we go down for OT," Madeline said, "I'm going to say I have to pee. The bathroom in OT's getting fixed so they'll have to let me go in the RT room. I saw somebody do it yesterday. Nobody's in that room then. They just watch you from the OT door. I'm going."

(If you close your eyes and listen very hard you can actually hear, through years and miles, my fifteen-year-old brain creaking forward like a long dormant watermill while I process this massive amount of new and confusing information.)

"To the bathroom?" I asked.

She looked at me and rolled her eyes without rolling her eyes. That was something she could do. Then she lit a cigarette even though she had one burning in the ashtray. Sometimes between us we had four or five cigarettes going at once, sitting in ashtrays around her room. We just kept lighting them. Cigarettes were the only thing we had enough of. Our parents brought cartons and cartons of them to the hospital. It was all they could give us. It was all we wanted.

"*Going* going?" I said. "Where?"

"To get some pills," she said. "There's that Walgreens up the road."

"You should brush your hair," I said. "So they think you're a regular person."

"A lot of regular people don't brush their hair," she said.

"I don't think you know how fucked up your hair is," I said.

On this point I am absolutely clear: there was no need for her to explain what she was going to do with those pills. We had discussed ideal dosage, blend, timing, technique, at length. I had failed before; we had both failed before; but we were not going to fail again. She had learned from others' successes. She had been schooled by the best teachers in the finest institutions. Here in the world of healing, pills were locked away in vaults, like treasure. Out in the world, in brightly lit stores, they lay across aisles in white boxes for the taking. You only had to know which boxes to choose.

About the deaf man. About the Big Macs. About the vampires

in white coats who sucked your blood while you ate breakfast with your free arm. About the mouth checks. About fielding grounders in the hall on New Year's Eve. About the lighter on the wall. About the lady who thought every door was a door to outside.

■■■　■

Madeline and I had made numerous precious keepsakes in OT in our several months together. We'd made moccasins from kits, molded clay into vases, hooked rugs, stitched pillows. We'd painted fruit and landscapes and each other. We'd made photo collages using old issues of *Good Housekeeping* and *Better Homes and Gardens,* snipping out the pictures with children's scissors. It was like kindergarten, OT, except someone always frisked you before you returned to the unit because there were countless things in the OT room that you could kill yourself with given a little ingenuity and about three minutes alone.

We took some hollowed-out watercolors and set up at a table by ourselves, as far removed from the other patients as we could get. This is what we normally did—we did not wish to be hassled by the RT staff to have positive interactions with others—but it was especially important on this day so that we could confirm and execute our plans discreetly.

"How long will you need?"

"As long as possible," she said. "You've got to give me a good head start. Five minutes if you can."

"You'll have to run like hell," I said.

"I can run like hell," she said. "I was on the track team in middle school."

She had told me this before so I knew it was true, but looking at her now it was hard to believe she could make it up a single flight of stairs. She also once told me a story about when she was at another hospital and she had cramps and her roommate had tied pillows to her with bed sheets, in strategic places to combat the cramps, and then the roommate had gone to breakfast and Madeline had lain in her bed with pillows tied to her for nine hours until someone had come to get the roommate's stuff because the roommate had swallowed seven Parcheesi pieces and had been transferred to a different ward. That was a different kind of hospital than this one. In this hospital they came into your room every thirty minutes overnight and shined a flashlight on you to make sure you were resting comfortably. In this hospital they kept you busy with moccasin kits and Ping-Pong and memory games. In this hospital they looked toward the future, including weekly "exit strategy" meetings during which you dutifully mapped out the rest of your life and talked about how you were going to pay your electric bill and keep your bathroom tidy. In that other hospital there was no pretending about the rest of your life or your tidy bathroom.

"Good luck," I said. And I meant it. In that moment there was no part of me I could reach that did not want her to succeed.

"Good luck to you," she said. And she meant it, too.

About the man who went after his own face with a plastic fork. About the slices of light in the solarium. About the woman who always forgot how to play Go Fish. About sitting in the lockers. About where we carved our names. About the glazed doughnuts. About her sweater.

(My god—her sweater! What but history held it together? It was as ratty as her hair, hanging in the same twisted mess. Did it survive?

Was it in a drawer somewhere in Illinois? Could I use it as a lap blanket, sitting here now, today?)

There were three staff in the OT room, two actual occupational therapists, smiley Nancy and anxious Linda, and a college girl who was busy discovering she didn't want to pursue this as a career after all. Madeline went up to smiley Nancy. I couldn't hear what she said but then she went through the door into the RT room and smiley Nancy hovered around the door, cheerfully delivering unreturned smiles from table to table. I slid off my stool and approached her.

"I want to do a paint by number," I said. "Can you help me find one?"

"Why don't you ask Sabrina?" she said. Apparently Sabrina was the college girl.

"I don't know her," I said. "I just—" Nancy glanced toward the closed bathroom door in RT. And then I knew what I had to do. I had to smile. But how to organize my face into a smile? Lips up, I thought, but then I felt my lips purse instead of smile. At the ends, I thought. Lips up at the ends. But how to change the angle of your lips? Then I remembered: the cheeks. Yes, it was all in the cheeks. Just a little push with the cheeks. My lips were chapped and I felt the bottom one split just a bit in the center and that was how I knew I had succeeded. There it was. Nancy's smile grew, reflecting mine.

"Can you help me find it?" I asked again.

"Oh, hon," she said. "I can't tell you how nice it is to see that smile on your face."

I held onto it, desperately. It was like trying to hold onto a terrified cat.

"I know a lot of people in your life who have missed that pretty smile," Nancy said. "I know your mother would give—"

"Can you please help me find it?" I asked. "The paint by number?"

"Sure I can." She signaled to Sabrina. "Madeline's in the bathroom. Keep an eye?"

Sabrina did not exactly take up the post by the door. She just moved to that end of the room, glanced into RT, then started picking some polish off her thumbnail. I thought how Sabrina and Madeline were probably about the same age. Long before I met her Madeline had gotten into Grinnell and gone for a month but then she came home and went back in the hospital and that was that.

Nancy opened the paint-by-number cabinet. Three towering stacks of cardboard boxes loomed. All those teeny-tiny eights and elevens and seventeens, woodlands and shores and windmills and sunsets, just waiting to be filled.

"I want the horse one," I said.

"I don't think there is a horse one," she said. She peered at the boxes. I could tell she didn't want to actually look through them. She slid one off the top of the box tower. "What about the dolphin?"

"Linda told me there was a horse one," I said.

Anxious Linda was at a nearby table, helping a trembling old lady string together some moccasins she would never wear.

"Linda, there's a horse one, right?" I said. "You said there was a horse one, right? Right?"

Anxious Linda drifted toward us.

"Is there a horse one?" Nancy asked.

"A horse what?"

"Wait, it wasn't Linda," I said. "It was Sabrina." I looked down the room. "Sabrina?"

Sabrina took a few steps toward us, then a few more. Now there was no one watching the bathroom door. Now the coast was clear.

"What are you looking for?"

"The horse one," I said. "There it is."

I yanked a box out of the middle of one of the stacks and about fifteen boxes fell at our feet. We all looked at the one in my hand.

"That's a deer, hon," smiley Nancy said.

"Let me in there," anxious Linda said.

Then they were digging, all three of them. I had done it! If only she had been there to see it, to congratulate me. And then— amazing—smiley Nancy came up with a horse paint-by-number and I sat down by myself to work on it.

About the doorbell. About the corn nuts. About that last stupid jigsaw puzzle.

Three or four minutes later the door burst open and Nancy and Linda were called away. They went out into the hall. I smiled inside, my organs splitting just a tiny bit in the center, imagined she was halfway to the Walgreens by now, her middle-school track form returning with each stride. Maybe she was already standing at the counter. Maybe she had her money out. Maybe she had the pills in her hand. Maybe she.

Nancy and Sabrina came back in, tight-lipped. They looked at me, then looked away, then looked again.

"This is really hard," I said, setting down my brush. I had filled in the horse's left ear. "The boxes are too small. Can I go back up to the unit?"

Once she told me about a friend of hers who OD'd and died flat on her back by choking on her own vomit. It was a nasty way to go, Madeline said. Instead of slipping away peacefully you basically drowned in your own spit and acid. She said when she did it she would remember to roll onto her side, so if she puked, she wouldn't drown in it. She said you never knew for sure what you might need to remember, so you should remember everything.

■■■ ■

The door buzzed and we walked into the unit and there was Madeline, sitting at a table, a beefy orderly on one side and a nurse on the other. When she saw me she rolled her eyes without rolling her eyes.

Story goes she was only halfway down the hall when she ran into Brenda, the music therapist, who karate chopped and tripped her and then put her in a half nelson and called on her little walkie-talkie for help.

I went over to the table and sat down across from her.

"Hey," she said. There was a cup of cranapple juice in front of her and she took a sip.

"Hey," I said. "What's going on?"

"They're trying to take me over there," she said.

("Over there" = seclusion. Strapped in your special chair all day, then strapped in your bed all night. Straps to straps, for as long as they say. I had been strapped down once, only for one night, when I broke the thermostat off the wall and pulled out its insides just to see if it might explode like a hand grenade. You think it's just going to be one strap, but it's three, one like a belt around you, and then one on each side of the belt strapping you to the bedframe, so not only can you not get out of bed, but you can't lie any way but flat on your back. It was just one night, but in the morning only the top layer of me got up, peeled in a thin strip from the softball player, who stayed in the bed forever.)

"Why?" I asked. I turned to the nurse. "Why?"

"Doctor's orders," the nurse said. The nurse's name was Cindy. She always looked tired. One time she saw a picture of my dog, the only picture I kept in my room, and she talked to me for like ten hours about her golden retriever.

"I'm not going," Madeline said. "I want to stay here."

"You should have thought of that before," the nurse said. She didn't say it like a bitch, though. She said it like she was genuinely sorry Madeline hadn't thought of it before.

"I'm not going," Madeline said. "You guys can't make me go." (This would have been hilarious under any other circumstance. We might have laughed about it later if we'd had the chance.) "I'm staying here with my friend."

"I killed it down there," I said. "I gave you like ten minutes."

"Good job," she said.

"Let's go," the beef said.

"I'm not going," she said.

"You're going," he said. He took hold of her arm and she looked at me wildly.

"Do something," she said through clenched teeth.

I was frozen in my chair. *Do something?* Like what, exactly? Resistance was futile and would only result in straps to straps for us both. Another orderly came through the door and headed toward us. This one was scrawny.

"Take her other arm," beefy told scrawny.

Scrawny took her other arm and Madeline started kicking frantically. Everybody in the solarium turned around and watched. It was good clean fun. Two more orderlies came running.

"Do something!" she screamed at me. It was an ugly, frantic sound and nothing like her.

"Don't hurt her," I said. I said it quietly but firmly. "Please stop. You're hurting her."

"Do something!"

Then they really had her, one on each limb. Like I said, she was tiny, rail thin, so even thrashing wildly it didn't take much for them to contain her. The nurse and I watched her go. They carried her off like an animal.

The cranapple juice was still sitting on the table. Somehow it hadn't spilled in all the commotion. I stood up and swiped it off the table with my hand and it splashed all over the floor. Cindy the nurse made a little sound, "ooh," and I turned to her triumphantly. But she just looked sad.

"I'm not cleaning it up," I said.

"I'll get it," she said. And she did.

■■■ ■

Would it have made any difference, what I did or didn't do that day, to the rest of her life? Would it have made any difference, what I did or didn't do that day, to the rest of mine?

Story goes she went from seclusion to another hospital, and then another. I sent her a letter and she sent me a postcard back and the writing was shaky. But then things got better for her. She went home, and was there for a few months and started thinking about going back to college. Story goes she even packed her bags. It was the end of summer and she was all registered for classes. Then one morning her mother came into her room and she wasn't there and they went looking for her. They must have known right away, as soon as they saw she was gone, what had happened. Story goes they found her in a field. On her back or on her side, I don't know.

Once she told me about a guy she knew at that other hospital who had found a yellow construction hard hat, left behind in a re-done bathroom. The guy put on the hard hat and walked out into the unit and went up to a nurse he didn't know and asked where the exit was. The nurse showed him to the door, entered the code, and let him out. The guy walked about a mile until he got to a gas station. He went inside and bought a sandwich, and then he sat on the curb in front of the gas station with his feet in a puddle and ate the sandwich. Then he walked back to the hospital and went up the stairs to the unit and rang the buzzer, because he didn't really have anywhere else to go. He just wanted to see if he could get away with it. And he could. Because under the right circumstances, Madeline said, even a crap disguise could be your ticket out. She said this was one of those things you might need to remember.

And so I have.

SHELTER

More often than not it happens like so: in the middle of the night I'm woken up by a car door slamming out front. Usually the car's idling and there's a little bit of radio playing and sometimes there's a whistle or tongue click or scuffle. Not often words. People come alone mostly, and people who do what they're doing aren't the kind of people who'd have words for a dog, though every so often someone'll say a "sorry" or a "see ya" before getting back into the car and driving away. When I can tell they're good and gone I pull out of bed and, unless it's winter, open up the front door in my nightie and bare feet and usually the dog's standing about where it was dropped, wagging its tail and looking up the road after the car, not getting the picture entirely, and I rattle my jar of Milk-Bones and nine times out of ten the mutt'll turn and run right up to me, and I let it stay in the house until morning, so it don't have to go meet all the others out back in the kennel in the middle of the night. They're barking by now, of course—they bark all the time, once one starts they all gotta be heard—but the sound is as

53

familiar to me as crickets or trucks on the highway, so I hardly hear it anymore.

I've found families for somewhere near four hundred homeless dogs across the state of New Hampshire. For twenty-five years I answered the phone for Dr. Brick, the town vet, but when Doc retired I looked around and saw I was fifty-two and had lots of days left and no clear way to fill them. I was still living in the house I'd grown up in, the mortgage long since settled. And I had a little money saved, so I didn't need a job that would pay much, if anything. I'd seen lots of hard-luck dogs in my years with Dr. Brick, strays brought in by folks who'd found but couldn't keep them, healthy, good dogs taken down (sometimes by me, in the back of my station wagon) to the shelter where I knew damn well they'd be gassed in a matter of weeks. So it seemed like maybe this was a way I could fill those days.

I've been at it nearly a decade now, so a lot of people know I do what I do, and if all a person wants is a regular old dog—not one to show or train for some job or another—they might call me instead of going to a pet store or a puppy mill. Then what I do is I go out to the person's house, check things over to make sure they've got the right kind of space and the right reasons to be looking for a dog— that they're not the type to lose interest or change their minds after a week or two, landing the dog right back where it started—and then once they've signed the papers I let them come out to my place and take their pick from the lot. For the picking, the dogs line up against the kennel fence, slapping tails and nosing through the holes. A few hang back, some shy, others seeming not to care, scratching at a flea or stretching out in the sunshine, like they don't give a damn who wants them and never did.

Twenty dollars is all I ask as payment, enough to buy a couple more bags of the store-brand food for the ones left behind. Some people give me more. One time a lady from Hanover wrote me a check for five hundred dollars. She said I was doing the lord's work. I thought to myself that maybe the lord had more important things to worry about than a kennel full of slobbering dogs, but I wasn't about to say so, standing there with her check in my hand. The truth was, I didn't really know why I did what I did, and I didn't see any reason to spend a whole lot of time thinking about it. It was just the way it was.

I've gotten through a lot by not overthinking things, by being able to keep certain matters out of my mind. You busy yourself with living, however it is you choose to busy yourself—dogs or kids or broken cars or numbers in a book—and you might well forget that after a year of anticipation your father decided not to move the family to Florida after all, or that the man you almost married had a change of heart at the last minute and traded you in for another. My sister, who lives down in Boston, thinks all the time about everything and as a result takes a half dozen pills every morning. Last year I watched her suffer every detail of her daughter's wedding and I thought: *you can have it.* And so when I felt that thing while I was soaping in the shower, that thing like an acorn, I just put it right out of my mind. I went on tending to my dogs and making home visits and doing what I do and I went so far as to cancel my yearly checkup with Dr. Lands because I knew once I had that paper gown on there would be no more not thinking about it. And one day in October, when I was starting to feel a little weak walking from the house to the kennel and the acorn wasn't an acorn anymore but a walnut, I drove up to the top of my dirt drive and swung shut the rusty iron gate and put a sign on the bars that said CLOSED—DO NOT DROP

DOGS. Because I had twenty-seven dogs in the kennel and I had to find homes for all of them before I was dead.

■■■ ■

It was a week or so later, around about Halloween, that I got a call from a man named Jerry who said he'd read about my kennel in his local newspaper and wanted to get one of my dogs. A big dog, he said.

"Not tall and bony," he said over the telephone. "Stocky. Fat if you have one. Do you?"

"Sure," I said. "I got all kinds." They were barking out back as we spoke.

"I'd like to see them immediately." He talked swift and clipped like a military man, everything an order. "I'll be there at three o'clock."

I hesitated, but not for more than a breath or two. I needed to place the dogs in a hurry, sure, but I had to stick to the rules. What did the dogs care about a little lump? All they wanted was somebody who'd take them and keep them. So I told this Jerry I would have to make a home visit first, and if he passed then he could come out and take his pick.

"I'll bring references," he said. "There's no need for—"

"This is the way it works," I said. "No home visit, no dog."

He didn't say anything for a minute, but I could tell he was still there. I could practically hear the spokes in his head creaking through the telephone line. Then he said, "Just you? Nobody else?"

"There is nobody else," I said.

And so he gave me directions to his house, up in Cornish, about forty miles from my town. We set a time for the following morning.

■■■ ■

One day last year I did a home visit in New London and I was walking through the house and I saw an old man sitting in an easy chair and I knew right off he was dead. His hands were droopy in his lap in a way only dead hands droop. So I said to the woman walking me around—she wanted a little dog, one that would sit on her lap while she did the crossword—I said, "Ma'am is that man okay?" even though I knew full well he wasn't, but didn't know quite how to say it. And she said, "Oh, Daddy always takes his nap around this time," and instead of telling her that her father was dead as a doornail I just said "oh, all right." And I guess a little while after I left she must have figured it out. I don't know what exactly happened because she never did call me about getting a little dog.

Lying in bed that night before I went out to Jerry's, I started thinking of that old man and his droopy hands. I tried to imagine the way my body would relax when I went, in which direction my head would nod, where my eyes might be fixed before somebody had a chance to shut them. When my mother died, down at the hospital in Manchester, frail as a leaf, she gave a little gasp of surprise right before the end. I wondered if anything would surprise me, if I would think something different than I'd thought before.

Then I pushed all that garbage out of my mind and went to sleep.

■■■ ■

There was a gate at Jerry's driveway, with a little box like at Wendy's. I poked the button and a crackly woman came on and I told her who I was and she sighed and said, "Come on up." And the gate swung open and I pulled through. And right then an idea started coming to me that these were people who could take three or four of my dogs. There must have been ten acres of grass and trees from what I could see and every bit of it fenced. The house was just shy of a mansion, two stories with tall windows and long white steps leading to a front porch that was empty but big enough to hold twenty rocking chairs. I parked my car at the foot of those stairs and saw Jerry was waiting for me up on the porch. He was older than he'd sounded on the phone. He looked eighty, though he also looked like he'd be okay with a few big dogs, tall and spry and with those muscled forearms you always find yourself looking at a moment too long. He had a head full of gray hair that was going in a hundred directions and a rectangle chin. There was no sign of the woman who'd sighed into the box.

"You gotta lot of room for a dog to run," I called to him as I got out of the car.

"I don't want a dog to run," he said, crossing those arms as I climbed the steps toward him. "I want a dog to lie on my feet."

"Most dogs'll want to run every so often," I said, reaching the top. My words came out thin and wheezy. It was weary work, climbing, and I wasn't sure how many stairs I had left in me.

"Don't you have a fat, old dog?"

I gathered my breath. "Sure I do. I got a few of 'em in fact. But even fat, old dogs need to get up every so often."

He twisted his lips into a lopsided frown. He looked like a child when he did it, a young child experimenting in the bathroom mirror with what his own face could do, and I nearly busted out laughing.

"What is it you need to see?" he asked.

By now, frankly, I was more than a little curious. I'd been to a lot of houses, met a lot of people. And I know they say everyone's different, that we're just like snowflakes, no two alike and all that, but I think that's a load. I think most people are alike. I think most people go from the job to the TV to the pillow. In between are meals and a quick game of catch or checkers and a telephone call and one minute of looking out the window wondering what happened to someone.

But there was something about Jerry that wasn't like a person you met coming and going, something about the way he was old and young all at once. Plus, if I was going to talk him into taking more than one of my dogs (four was the number I had in my head right then), I was going to have to warm him up a little bit first.

"I need to look inside," I said. "I need to see where the dog'll be kept."

"The dog will be kept in the dungeon," he said. "And forced to wear a clown costume."

"Listen, you'd be surprised," I said. "I've had some real weirdos. Once I—"

"No need for stories," he said, opening the door.

I figured he must have just been moving in. The first two rooms we entered—what might have been a living room and dining room— were empty of furniture, the walls peeling paint. Our footsteps on the wood floors echoed all the way to the high ceilings.

"Where you comin' from?" I asked. "Out of state?"

"Pardon?"

I gestured to the emptiness. "I'm guessin' you just bought the place?"

"I've lived here for fifty years," he said. "So it depends on your definition of 'just.'"

In the kitchen there was a breakfast-nook-type area with a small circle table and two wood chairs. There was nothing on the counters, and I don't mean there were no plates or cups or cereal boxes. There was just *nothing*—no toaster or sugar bowl or roll of paper towels. The only thing in the whole room that would have moved in an earthquake were two dog bowls in the corner by the fridge. One of the bowls was filled to the rim with water.

"You got a dog already?" I asked. "Lookin' for a pal?"

"No dog." He cleared his throat. "Just the bowls so far."

"A dog needs bowls, all right," I said.

"Then you're satisfied. I can—"

"Just one more thing," I said. "I need to see where the dog will sleep. Some people, they—"

He held up his hand. "No stories," he said.

He led me to a small room off the kitchen. If it hadn't been connected by wood and plaster you couldn't have convinced me it was part of the same house. First off, it was tiny compared to everything else—maybe it had been a laundry room or a mud porch. But now it was carpeted with thick brown shag and stuffed with furniture: a fat brown recliner, a rickety old tray table, and one of those big fancy TVs with cables and speakers and slots for movies and whatnot. *The Andy Griffith Show* was playing on the TV. There was an open jar of pickles and three cans of ginger ale on the tray table, and at least four or five socks flopped on the floor like dead fish.

"This is where it'll sleep?"

"I expect so," he said. "It's where I spend most of my time."

No kiddin', I thought. But instead I said, "Are there others in the household?"

"Possibly," he said, taking a small step away from me. "But they won't have anything to do with the dog. The dog will be my responsibility."

He said this like he was repeating something he'd been told a bunch of times, and I thought again that he was like a gray-haired boy. Here he stood, seventy-five, eighty years old, and I could imagine that crackly woman on the intercom saying to him, "I'm not feeding that dog, not walking that dog, not brushing that dog. You bring a dog into this house you better be willing to take care of it, buster." And Jerry toeing the floor, like little Opie Taylor on TV, saying, "Oh yes, ma'am, I'll take care of it, I promise."

"Here's the thing," I said. "There's paperwork you gotta fill out, and there's a form that needs signed by everyone in the household. I don't want a dog coming back to me because someone here doesn't want it."

"I won't return the dog," he said.

"I know you're thinking that's true," I said. "I know you—"

"I won't return the dog," he said angrily. "No matter what."

"You feel that way now," I said. "But you might change your mind if there's someone harping on you about it every time it makes a noise or sheds some fur. Everyone has to sign off on the form. Everyone. No form, no dog."

He scowled. "I'll be in touch," he said.

■■■ ■

Here's a fact: nobody wants a dog in November. Spring's the best— no surprise there—and summer's fine and early fall calls to mind pictures of happy dogs playing in leaf piles and even December brings out a few folks looking for a Christmas present. But nobody in the state of New Hampshire's thinking about dogs those first weeks of bitter cold, leading up to Thanksgiving, when the threat of snow sits over every house big and small and it's only a matter of time before simple things—getting to work, picking up groceries—aren't so simple.

Not that I didn't knock myself out trying. I spent extra money for color ads in the local paper, taped signs in every store window, waived the twenty-dollar fee. This brought out a couple more people than usual, and after the home visits and the paperwork I was down to sixteen dogs by the middle of November. But I had to move faster. At this rate it would take well into the new year to find spots for them all, and I was pretty sure I didn't have that long.

My sister called, asking me to come down to Boston for Thanksgiving, but I told her I was too busy. I might have gone—there was something nice even thinking about it, a heavy meal and voices talking over each other and a football game on somewhere—but I was afraid if I went I would buckle and tell her about what was inside me, and I knew right where that would lead. By the time that turkey's bones were simmering for soup I'd be in some specialist's office and there'd be cousins and nieces and god knows who turning up with flowers.

"Some day I'm just gonna come up there and kidnap you," she said. "All alone in the old house with those dogs out back, it's not right. You come live near me and we'll go for lunch every day and play bridge with the other ladies on the block. Two sisters growing old together."

"What'll Joe think of that?"

"What Joe thinks of everything—that he should turn up the TV."

We'd thought, for almost a year when I was twenty-three and

she was twenty-one, that her and I and the men we were fixing to marry would take vacations together, play shuffleboard on the deck of a cruise ship, ride donkeys down the Grand Canyon.

"I miss you," she said. "You might as well be a million miles away."

"I'll see you soon," I said. "Not now, but soon."

■■■ ■

It was the next Friday, around lunchtime, when Jerry came out to my place. He drove a big pickup truck, shiny black and no more than a couple years old. He pulled past the dirt drive and onto the grass and on up to the kennel, which most people have the common courtesy not to do. He was already out of the truck and looking at the dogs by the time I'd gotten on my coat and gloves and made my way up there. He wasn't dressed for the weather—it was twentysomething degrees, I bet—and he had his hands tucked into the pits of his flannel shirt.

"Talked her into it, did ya?" I asked him.

He didn't look at me, just kept checking out the dogs. "Talked who into what?"

"The one who didn't want a dog. Promised her you'd take good care of it?"

He rubbed his hands together and then blew into them. "Are there any fatter ones?"

True, most of the outright strays were skin and bones. But there were at least three overweight dogs—orphaned by divorce or allergy most likely—standing not ten feet from him when he said this.

"Look at that black one," I said. A bit of dizziness blew through my head and I took hold of the fence pole to steady myself. "You want fatter than that?"

"He a barker?"

"They're dogs," I said. "They bark. But no, he's not one that keeps you up nights. That one in the corner—he's a fatty, too, and quiet. The two get on well. You want 'em both, I'll charge you just for the one."

He shook his head. "I don't want two dogs," he said. He still hadn't looked at me.

"You got a big yard, all fenced up. Shame to let it go to waste."

Now he finally turned. In the cold his face was a little gray, his eyes watery. "It's not going to waste," he said.

"Well," I said. "Come on down to the house and we'll write it up."

I was stalling, really. The sky promised snow and probably no one else would come by today, and though being alone wasn't something that'd bothered me for the last forty or so years, the truth was in the early afternoons it was starting to get to me just a little bit now. Plus maybe I could convince him if I gave him a cup of coffee. We walked down to the house. I hadn't been much for picking up in the last couple months, and there was a lot of mess around the living room, including a couple empty boxes that the bulk Milk-Bones had come in that I'd just left lying near the front door.

"You want a coffee?" I asked him, a little embarrassed by the state of things.

"You're moving," he said, looking around the room.

"No," I said. "I just—"

"You are. You're moving. I saw the sign on the gate." He pointed a bony finger at me. "You don't want any more dogs because you're moving down to Florida to live in a condominium. You're going to get skinny and leathery and wear shorts with flowers on them."

I laughed a little. "All right," I said. "Have it your way. Do you want a coffee or not?"

"You're not going to like it down there," he said. He sat down at my kitchen table, which was covered in junk mail and paper napkins.

"Now how could you know that? You don't even know my name."

"You're not going to like it," he said. "This is your home. Look at this place. Nobody in Florida lives like this."

"Where's your paperwork?" I asked. "In the truck?"

"I don't have it," he said. "And I'm not going to have it. But you're going to give me that fat black dog anyway, because you're moving to Florida and you want to get rid of those mutts as soon as you can."

I thought about making a deal. I thought about saying, okay, mister smarty-pants, take two, the black one and his pal, and I'll take your word for it that you won't change your mind, that you'll keep them no matter what that crackly woman might say. I thought about it for five or six seconds, probably, which is likely the longest I've taken someone's word for in thirty years. But then I remembered, and felt like a fool for forgetting: you never knew what a person will do. They'll tell you one thing and five minutes later do something else. I'd seen it again and again.

"She needs to sign," I said, pushing back from the table. "I'll get you another copy if you—"

"What will you do down there?" he asked. "Bingo?"

"You really got me all figured out," I said.

He finished his coffee and set the cup down on some yellowed envelopes. "Do you know who I am?" he asked.

"Sure," I said. "You're a rich man with a fenced yard big enough for a half dozen dogs who's afraid to ask a woman to sign a piece of paper."

He scoffed. "And you're too scared to give me a dog without a guarantee. What do you care? You'll be sunning yourself by the time the dog knows which door he goes out to pee."

"My dogs," I said. "My rules."

■■■ ■

It's almost always something tiny that fouls things up, ruins your plans big or small. A couple days later I was at the grocery store and feeling a little woozy. I hadn't been eating very good, had been sick to my stomach if I put much more in there than a few cookies, so sometimes I swayed a bit on my feet and had to find a spot to sit. So I was pulling out a bag of dog food from the bottom shelf and I felt that wave wash over me and stood up and then all the colors came rushing at me at once and that's the last I remember.

"Ma'am," the nurse said. "Do you know where you are?"

Well, I thought, I'm looking at a gal in a nurse's uniform, so unless it's Halloween I guess I'm at the hospital. But I didn't say this, only nodded.

"You hit your head," she said. She was a black gal, cute, with the braids in her hair. "Do you remember?"

I nodded again. What I was trying to figure was if they'd already given me the once-over. I was thinking, by the look on her face, that they probably had.

"The doctor will be back shortly," she said. "Just stay here and rest."

■■■ ■

"The place is only two miles from my house," my sister said.

In the hospital room there were cards and flowers and bright balloons bobbing in the corners, all the things I'd been hoping I could be spared.

"I can come up every afternoon," she said. "It's the best care in Boston, which you know means the best care anywhere. There's a lake with ducks. And the big goldfish."

"I'm sure it's nice," I said. I was watching the local news, on the television way up high. I'd turned off the sound but I knew well enough what they were saying, and all in all it was better than anything coming out of my sister's mouth.

"A man came today while I was packing," she said.

I turned away from the news lady. "Did he take a dog?"

"He didn't come for a dog. He came for you. You got a boyfriend you didn't tell me about?"

"Who was it?"

"He didn't say. He brought you this." She handed me a beach towel. It had a flaky picture of a golden retriever on it. It was one of those towels you might get at Kmart, rough to the touch, ready to fall apart the first time you put it in the washer.

"He said you could take it to Florida with you, to remember your dogs. I said you must be thinking of somebody else. My sister's not going anywhere. I said . . ."

"Don't," I said. I turned back to the TV. The weather map was bright blue with snow. "I don't want to know what you said."

"Well, I'm sorry if I talked out of turn. I didn't have a clue in the world who he was and why he was bringing you a present. It didn't occur to me until he was driving off that he might be your—"

"He was just a man who was thinking about a dog," I said.

"He seemed awfully sorry to hear about your trouble."

I kept my eyes on the TV. "That what he said?"

"No," she admitted. "He didn't say anything. He just *seemed*. Then he took his truck and left. But I guess he still wanted you to have this, even after I told him about . . ."

She held the towel out to me.

"Just pack it away with everything else," I said.

"Why don't I leave it for now?" she said, tucking it beside me. "I'll just leave it in case."

■■■ ■

That night I wrote him a postcard. I still had his address from when I'd gone up to his house. I was thinking twelve dogs was better than thirteen. I was thinking all the guarantees in the world didn't mean anything. I'd had a life full of them now, paperwork stepping-stones from the time I was twenty-four all the way to this hospital bed. And now I could see the path in front of me, down to Boston, and then the end of it.

I had that rough towel across my cold knees.

"Jerry," I wrote on the card. "Take the black one. I trust you won't bring it back."

■■■ ■

Yesterday my sister came to tell me the dogs had run off.

"I'm so sorry," she said. "When I got there the kennel gate was standing open and they were all gone, every one of them. I'm sorry, honey. I know—"

"It's all right," I said, patting her hand. "There's nothing you could do."

"I bet they'll get taken in," she said. "Some of them, at least. They're good dogs. They'll find homes on their own, honey. They'll find little boys who—"

"Shhhh," I said, because I could hear something in the distance, gravel crunching under tires, claws scraping on metal, a man cursing me. I smiled. I could see it now, clear as day: the gate hanging open, the dust kicking up, thirteen dogs crowded in the bed of that black truck. Old Jerry was scowling. Where were they all gonna sleep? And what was he supposed to tell that woman? He was going to have to do some fast talking, that was for sure, but he'd work it out. He'd been living in that big empty house for fifty years. Once he was set on something, he wasn't the type to change his mind.

WHY THEY RUN THE WAY THEY DO

Ginny, the cleaning woman, knows what I've been up to. How could she not? For almost two years I've been bumping into her after midnight, at least twice a week; she looks up from her vacuuming or polishing, smiles congenially but not warmly, then returns to her work. Sometimes she's on the elevator when I get on, and we ride down eighteen floors in silence to the gaping, vacant lobby. Sometimes she's got a bag of trash that's bigger than she is, and I wonder how she's possibly going to get it to the dumpster. But my purse is heavy and I have wadded underwear in my pocket and I have to be back in this building in six or seven hours, so I don't offer to help. When I feel guilty about this, I remind myself that cleaning is her *job*, that she wouldn't walk past the reception desk at Wrona, Blake, Mulcahey and Kramer Law Assoc. and see me juggling six impatient clients and offer to lend a hand.

"Do you really think she knows?" Donald (he's the Mulcahey) asks me. We are on the foldout in his office and he's shuffling his feet around under the covers trying to locate his socks.

"I don't know," I say, though of course I know, of course she knows, of course everybody in the office knows, and probably half the people in the damn building, not that they care. But Donald lives under the delusion that we are being discreet, that if we don't leave the premises together at 2:00 a.m. or make extended eye contact during working hours that no one will be the wiser, and I allow him to enjoy this delusion because if he knew all the people who know, it would make him sweat. And he's a big man, and he doesn't need to sweat any more than he does already.

∎∎∎ ∎

"One of these days he's just going to keel over," Tommy says, clutching his chest and tipping over onto the couch. "And then what're you gonna do? You'll have to get him off that foldout bed, prop him up at his desk with a pen—"

"Okay," I say. "Enough."

"You'll have to *dress* him." He howls with laughter. "You're going to have to ask that housekeeper to help you. The two of you are going to have to—"

"Okay," I say. "I get it. You can stop now."

"Just don't call me," he says, grabbing a fistful of Cheetos. "I don't want any part of it."

On nights I do not stay late at the office, Tommy and I sit in my apartment in sweats and slippers and watch television for hours and hours. It is hard to find a friend who loves TV as much as you do, who is not ashamed to admit that he watches television for six to eight hours every single day, that he watches truly indiscriminately, moves seamlessly from *Gilligan's Island* to the History channel, from *Seinfeld* (the seventh or eighth viewing of most episodes) to *Nightline,* talk shows, game shows, reruns of *old* game shows, decorating shows, C-Span, soaps, even the occasional sporting event. We watch without excuses, without pretexts or apologies, without fear of judgment. We just watch. Christ, do we watch.

(Devoted Gay Friend + Adulterous Affair = Simplicity and Contentment.)

■■■ ■

Tommy's partner of four years, Gil, is a doctor. He's one of these appallingly high-energy people, works in the ER, almost exclusively the graveyard shift. This plays out well for all of us. When I am at work Tommy is with Gil. When Gil is at work Tommy is with me. When both Gil and I are at work, Tommy rides his bike. To see him splayed across my couch in the evenings, his hand buried in a bag of Cool Ranch Doritos, you would never know he logs forty miles every morning. He is a competitive racer. He was in the Olympic trials when he was eighteen. Now he competes in local races where he wins trophies and gift certificates to Applebees. He doesn't have a job. He defines himself not as independently wealthy, but as independently comfortable. And except for his racing gear, he and Gil can live off what Gil makes at the hospital.

■■■ ■

The fourth letter from Mariela arrives on a Monday. Donald flashes me a glimpse of the flimsy gray airmail envelope when he passes me after lunch; he is bursting with excitement, but it is a rule that we can not open the letter until the office is closed and we can do it alone, without fear of interruption. At 5:00 Donald sends me the official signal that he can stay late—he opens his door halfway. This means I should go kill a few hours, until much of the office has cleared out, and then return. Sometimes I go to the movies, the rush-hour special, though because I am still in my work clothes—fitted blouse, gabardine pencil skirt, heels—the movie feels like another part of my job, and I find myself sitting unnaturally straight and smiling pleasantly regardless of what is on the screen.

Mariela was Donald's anniversary gift to me. When we had been together one year he presented me with her picture and her paperwork. She is ten years old and lives in an orphanage in Paraguay. Every month we send her twenty-eight dollars (less than a cup of coffee a day!) to help pay for her food and clothes and school books.

"This is our little girl," he'd said that night, touching the photo with tender fingertips. "Look at her, Lauren. She's ours, yours and mine."

Donald and his wife have three children, two in high school and one in college. They pose on his desk in matching silver frames.

"Isn't she beautiful?" he'd said, squeezing my hand until the blood stopped at my knuckles. "She's all ours. She's nobody else's. She's yours and mine."

That was a little over a year ago. And the truth was, it had totally creeped me out in the moment. I didn't tell him this, because he was so obviously moved by it, so blown away by his own gesture, but the whole idea of it made me queasy. Weren't we using her, this innocent little brown orphan? Wasn't she an accomplice to something torrid and dirty? But then, almost overnight, it seemed perfectly acceptable, just as most everything in my life that had ever made me inconveniently queasy (i.e.: my parents' grisly divorce, my absurd broken engagement in college, my temp-job career) had swiftly morphed into *perfectly acceptable*. After all, I told myself, it wasn't as if we had taken Mariela from someone else, someone more deserving. Before us she had nothing, and now she had twenty-eight bucks a month and she meant something to someone. So I have grown used to the idea that she is out there—out there and ours—and Donald and I devour the letters with equal pleasure. She is, I am quite certain, the only child I will ever have. She has never barfed on me and she will never break my heart. And yet, when we hold her picture, surely what we are feeling is all the joy and pride of real parents.

She sends us actual letters. When I first heard about it, I imagined the letters would be something like the sweepstakes notices you get, the ones with your personalized information spliced in:

*Dear **Lauren and Donald**,*
*Thank you for your generous gift of **$28**. I used it to buy **a new goat**. Now there is milk for my classmates. I hope the weather in **Chicago** is pleasant.*

Sincerely,
Mariela

But I was wrong. The words are her own—translated, of course, and typed on a piece of flowery stationery:

Dear Family, (this new letter begins)
Today at school we talked about rivers and why they run the way they do. After school we played football even though it was raining. I was on the red team and I scored one goal and then a boy named Jorge who was on the green team rubbed

mud in my hair. Last week I was sick but I am getting better.
Thank you for writing me and helping me to have books and
clothes for school.

Love, Mariela

"Jorge better watch his back," Donald says. "I'm gonna kick his ass."

The agency has included an updated photo and we sit there on the foldout couch squinting at it, as if even in the photo the distance between us and Mariela is immense. She is standing on a gravel road in front of a squat building that I assume is the school, because she is holding two thick books pressed against her chest, in the same way I and many girls had held books at the age of ten, a shield that hid our bodies, the only thing we could hold so tightly at that age.

"She looks so old," I say. "She's not a little girl anymore."

"Soon she'll be casting spells on all the boys," he says. "Just like her mother." He pokes me in the ribs, a gesture I despise. I suspect he is one of those men who tickled his children until they begged for mercy, that he was so pleased with their laughter that he was able to overlook the dismay behind it.

"I'm not her mother," I say. "And Donald, your socks have holes in them, okay? You make a hundred and eighty—"

"You're as much her mother as anyone," he says, setting the letter aside.

"That's nice," I say. "I'm sure that would be a great comfort to her. You can't buy a week's worth of decent socks?"

"What's wrong, honey?" he asks. He puts his big palm on my cheek, a gesture I love, and I forget about his socks and Mariela. Sometimes I feel like I could sleep curled in his hand, like a hamster.

———

"Nothing," I say.

"No, really," he says. "What is it? Is it me?"

This is his favorite question: Is it me? Is it me?

■■■ ■

"Don't freak out," Tommy says. He is standing in my doorway with a supersize bag of BBQ Fritos. "Whatever you do, just don't freak out."

"What?" I say, closing the door. "What happened?"

"Just don't freak out."

"Okay, whatever, I won't freak out."

He sits down on the couch, picks up the remote, and turns off the television.

"I'm freaking out," I say.

"Me, too," he said. He pauses, then inhales and exhales deliberately like he is on an infomercial for yoga tapes. "We're moving."

"What do you mean, 'moving'?"

The word itself feels strange in my mouth. Moving. Moo-ving. A cow plus *ving*. You might say "I'm moving this couch to the other wall" or even "They're moving my office at work" but people themselves did not move. Things moved. Tommy and I have lived in this apartment complex for seven years, since literally the day after we graduated from college. When Tommy and Gil became a couple three years after that, Gil moved in; Tommy did not move out. Because Tommy did not move.

"Gil got this amazing offer to run the ER at this hospital in—"

"Gil?" I explode. "Since when is this about Gil? Since when is every goddamn thing about Gil?" The irony that Gil's name comes up approximately once a month, usually in passing, is popping around in the back of my brain like a Mexican jumping bean, impossible to grab.

"Sweetie," Tommy says miserably. And right then it becomes apparent that one of us is going to start crying. I'm not sure which of us, but either way it's something to be thwarted at all costs.

"Go home," I say. "I have stuff to do, all right? Just get out of here. I have like a million things to do."

He doesn't move from the couch. "Can I just turn on the TV instead?"

"Okay," I say. "Wanna Coke or something?"

"Okay," he says.

We drink our Cokes. We eat the Fritos down to the crumbs. We watch a special on the History channel about a British soldier in World War II who was dropped from an airplane, already dead, with bogus Top Secret documents in his pockets, sent to confuse the Nazis. It's always good, when you're feeling really lousy, to watch something about Nazis.

■■■ ■

Usually I skip the company picnic. Usually, as soon as the date is announced, I remember something very important that it conflicts with. This was true even before Donald and I were together. Didn't I see these people enough during the week? What did I need, exactly, with a bunch of tipsy lawyers and legal secretaries smeared with sunscreen and bug repellent, a bunch of kids running around screaming their heads off, their faces stained with watermelon? But this year an unfortunate turn of events has made it necessary for me to attend. I have won an award. In our annual client survey, the email marked "URGENT" informs me I have received an "unprecedentedly unanimous vote of 10 (excellent) for friendly customer service . . . both in person and on the telephone!"

"It's a big deal," Donald calls to me. He is standing in his private bathroom, in front of the mirror, poking a small red bump that has appeared below his left eye. "If you don't show up . . . well, it'll look really, really bad."

"You're telling me I might get fired for not coming to the company picnic?"

"I didn't say that." He pokes his head out the door. "Just . . . it'll be weird if you don't come. People might think it's because, you know, whatever."

"I might be sick," I said. "I might get the flu."

He's back at the mirror. Bug bite? Acne? Cancer? "Okay, it's dumb to you. Okay. Fine. But some people have been here for twenty years and never won something like this. It means something."

"Something besides I'm screwing the boss."

He abandons his prodding and comes out of the bathroom. "Are you kidding me? Really, Lauren, you think I had something to do with this? Is it that hard to believe that people think you do your job well?"

"I'm so proud," I say, twisting my heels into my shoes. "My college education has finally paid off. I think I'll call my mother. And imagine how proud Mariela will be when she hears."

"Babe, what is it?" he asks. "Is it me?"

"My friend Tommy is moving," I say. "In three weeks. He and Gil are moving to New Mexico."

"Wow," Donald said. He sits on the foot of the foldout beside me, puts his hand over mine. "But he's your best friend."

"I told him that. It didn't seem to make a difference."

"I'm really sorry," he says. And he is. He's not a bad guy. You hear about a guy like this, a guy—a *lawyer*, for crying out loud—banging his receptionist at the office two nights a week while his wife keeps his dinner warm, and you think you've got this guy all figured out. But you don't know that when he sees a spider crawling across his office wall, he'll catch it in a plastic cup and when he has a minute to spare he'll run the spider downstairs and shake it in one of the plants that line the front of our building.

"I'm sorry, too," I say.

■■■ ■

"You have to be my date," I tell Tommy the next night, during *Animal ER*. "You owe me big and I'm not going alone."

"Sure," he says. "I'll be your date. I'd love to be your date. Is Fatty going to be there?"

"He's not fat," I say. "Just because you weigh seventy pounds doesn't mean everyone else is fat."

"Ouch," Tommy says, because on TV a golden retriever is having a fishhook removed from his floppy ear. He changes the channel: *$100,000 Pyramid*, the real one, with Dick Clark.

"Yes!" we say, in unison.

"Is the wife coming?" he asks.

"Probably. I don't see why she wouldn't."

"What's her name again?"

"I don't know," I say, which is a lie. Her name is Carol. But I prefer to refer to her in my deliberate detached way as "the wife," the missus," or "the old ball and chain."

"I've never been to a company picnic before," Tommy says.

"Are you packing?"

"For the picnic? Too soon, I think."

"You're funny."

"I'm packing a little," he says. "You could come help, you know. We could hang out at my place."

We rarely hung out at his apartment. It smelled a little, I thought, like aftershave.

"I have more channels."

"This is true," he says. "I only have a hundred and five. We'd never be able to find anything to watch."

"New Mexico," I say. "Have you ever even been to New Mexico? Have you ever even been *through* New Mexico?"

"I've been to Arizona."

"I can't believe he's making you go. Of all the selfish—"

"He's not making me go," Tommy says. "It's exciting, okay? Going someplace new, starting over. I might even get a job myself. I'm ready for a change."

"Since when? Since last week? Since he *told* you you were ready for a change?"

"Lauren—" he says harshly. He starts to say something, then thinks better of it.

"What?"

"Nothing," he says.

We leave it at that. And I realize, as I turn back toward the TV, that I am all about *leaving it at that*. If I could *leave it at that* forever, if I could get away with never having another conversation of substance, with anybody, I might just take it and run.

Dear Family,

Today a dentist came to look at our teeth. He said mine were second best and all he did was give me a toothbrush. Some other kids had to have some teeth pulled and Jorge was one of them and his cheek swole up and everyone laughed at him. But I didn't. The dentist was a tall American man with a beard and one of the girls asked if he was Santa Claus. Then later somebody said that the dentist might adopt one of us so we all tried to guess who it would be. I think it will be the girl who asked if he was Santa Claus.

Thank you,

Mariela

"Poor Jorge," Donald says. It's the night before the company picnic and we are sitting on the middle of the foldout eating Chinese food from stained boxes. "Nobody's ever going to pick poor Jorge."

"I don't think anyone's going to pick any of them. After they're babies, nobody wants them."

"You never know," he says. "They might get lucky."

"Maybe I'll go get her."

"Who?"

"Mariela."

"Oh," he chuckles. "Right."

Of course I'm not even remotely serious, but as soon as he says "right" the whole thing racks into focus and makes more sense than any thought I've had in years.

"So what would you do?" I ask. "What would you do if I just showed up one day with her? Just one morning I come in to work and she's tagging along behind."

"Lauren," he says. "Come on. Cut it out."

"You started it," I say. "You're the one writing the checks. So what do you say? Let's go get her. We'll bring her back. She can live here in the office and we'll raise her. Two nights a week we'll order in pizza, rent some movies. The rest of the time she can just hang out around the building waiting for us to show up."

He looks weary. I know what he is thinking. Someone probably told him this would happen—one of the other lawyers, or his psychiatrist—that at some point the receptionist would get needy, go a little crazy, even, that at some point his joyride was going to end and the stakes were going to get higher and he was going to have to get rid of her somehow.

"I love you," he says. "Do you understand that? This isn't just like . . . a thing. I'm not like other people who do this. You know that, don't you?"

"I know," I say. "You're like . . . like you who does this."

"Tell me what to do," he says. "I need someone to tell me what to do."

■■■ ■

"That's the most pathetic thing I've heard in my entire life," Tommy says. "Jesus Christ, what a big baby."

We are on our way to the picnic. The sun is blazing in the sky. My feet are up on the dashboard and I realize I shaved only my left leg this morning. The end is near, I think. But what the hell? First you stop shaving your right calf, soon your fingernails grow ragged, eventually you stop brushing your teeth. Even the simplest matters of personal hygiene fall by the way. Next thing you know the health department is knocking on your door, and there you are on your couch, all alone, covered in bags of Doritos. And you, not even quite thirty. What happened to you?

"You're a little pathetic too," I tell Tommy. "Don't forget that. We're all a little pathetic."

"Exactly," he says. "Everybody gets to be a *little* pathetic. But you can't have more than your share, or there's not enough to go around. You can't be a hog about it."

■■ ■

The wife is adorable, cute as a shiny little button in that pushing fifty kind of way; her brown hair is bobbed, her makeup tastefully applied, her blouse bright and sleeveless, her walking shorts khaki and slimming. I can't think of a single bad thing to say about her, watching the two of them standing by the barbecue pits, standing close enough that their matching shorts brush against each other. Owning not a single outfit that falls between what I wear to work and what I wear in front of the television, I am grossly overdressed, despite my one stubbly leg.

"I should have worn my sweat pants," I say, trying to not allow my eyes to linger on the wife.

"You're making a statement," Tommy says. "You're telling the world that no occasion is too casual for heels. Soon women all over America will be playing softball in two-inch pumps."

I look at the schedule of events posted by the picnic tables, hoping that the awards ceremony is early on the agenda, that we can eat a quick burger and I can collect my prize (framed certificate, coffee mug) and be headed home inside of an hour. To my dismay I see that the ceremony comes last, after food, volleyball, and . . .

"Races!" Tommy says. "I didn't know there were *races!*"

I refuse the potato sack and egg-on-a-spoon, but after considerable badgering I agree to be Tommy's partner in the three-legged race, despite the fact that even with the heels kicked off my skirt promises to slow us down. Just before the starting gun—a teenager popping a Baggie—Donald and the missus hustle up to the starting line, all giggles and flushed faces. We are on one end of the line of competitors; they are on the other. Between us are three other couples who tumble into heaps barely out of the gate. Tommy drags me along; I fee like deadweight, and see Donald out of the corner of my eye, grimacing, trying to catch me. I believe in this moment he has forgotten who I am, so intent he looks upon winning the race. Tommy hurls himself through the blue-streamer finish line and drags me with him. We high-five and bounce off each other. We make complete fools of ourselves, long after it is appropriate. The wife comes over to congratulate us, and Donald comes panting along behind her, a slightly panicked look on his face.

"Congratulations," the wife says. "You're quite a pair."

"This is Lauren," Tommy says.

"Oh, the famous Lauren!" she says. "Congratulations on your award."

"Yes, congratulations!" Donald exclaims. He shouts it so loud his wife winces and gives him a look. "We're all very proud," he says at a normal level.

"Is this your husband?" the wife—Carol—asks.

"No," I say. "This is just Tommy."

■■■　■

In the car I completely dissolve. One moment we're sitting calmly at a red light and the next moment I'm blubbering.

"I can't believe you're actually going to leave me. I can't believe you're actually—"

"I'm not leaving you. For God's—"

"You stupid shit . . . mother . . . damn . . . freaking—"

"Good one," he says.

"Shut up," I say. "Don't you dare make me laugh, you—"

A horn blares behind us. The light has turned green. Tommy guns the engine and the car jolts into the intersection, shudders, chokes, and dies.

"Shit!" Tommy says, slamming the gearshift into park.

"What's wrong with it?"

"Stupid piece of—"

The horn blares again. "I know!" Tommy yells. "I know! Thank you very much!"

The guy whizzes around us and offers the predictable gesture. The car starts. Tommy puts it in drive and we move forward again, in silence. Tears eke out of my eyes and roll to the corners of my mouth. I am furious that I cannot stop them. We are only a mile from home when Tommy says:

"It does that sometimes when you give it too much gas. Dies at intersections."

"You should get that checked out," I say.

"I guess." He clears he throat, stares at the car in front of us. "Come to New Mexico," he says.

I sniffle ungracefully, lick the salt from my lips. "What?"

He glances at me briefly, then turns back to the road. "Come to New Mexico. Just do it. What do you have here?"

"You," I say.

"Yeah," he says. "And I'm going. So we could go together."

My tears have dried up. "All three of us? You, me, and Gil."

"Sure," he says. He pulls up in front of my apartment and turns off the car. "I mean, me and Gil. And . . . and me and you."

I take off my seat belt. I feel that Tommy and I are at the tail end of a very long date. I blow my nose before I turn to him.

"I think that's a little more than my share of pathetic," I say.

■■■ ■

On Monday I start packing my things at 4:45. I want to be standing in the elevator at 5:00, out of the building before Donald can signal me with his door. But then someone calls and I have to put them on hold forever and then a delivery man comes by with something stupid and important and then it's 5:05 and the office is almost empty and it's just me and a couple other girls and Donald's door is open halfway. I look at it, weigh my options. I think: *So my best friend has moved away. So what? It's not as if there's a dire shortage of fags who like TV and junk food. It's not as if anything* has *to change.*

"Come out for a drink?" one of the girls says.

Her voice so startles me that I literally flinch.

"Sorry," she says. "You wanna come out with us?"

"Me?" I say.

"Your boyfriend can come, too."

"Who?"

"From the picnic. He's cute."

"Yeah," I say. "Well, we have plans tonight."

And then they are gone and it's just me and Donald's door. And

I hear the girls' laughter down the hall and then I hear Ginny's vacuum cleaner start up in the office next door and I hear—don't I?—Donald on the phone with Carol telling her he's going to be late and I hear Tommy taping up his boxes and I hear the din of the television in my own apartment and my bag is packed and I'm out the door in the hallway and Ginny is there with her vacuum and the thick black cord is blocking my path.

"I'm not who you think I am!" I shout.

She turns off her vacuum. "Excuse me?"

"I'm not who you think I am," I say.

She smiles vaguely. "I'm sorry," she says. "Do I know you?"

I will go to Paraguay, I decide, as the elevator begins its descent. I will go to Paraguay, and I will never return. In the morning I will leave a note for Tommy, telling him what I have done, wishing him smooth pavement and two hundred channels in New Mexico. Then I will go to the airport and board a plane. By noon I will have cleared the airspace of my country and by dinnertime I will be on a bus on a gravelly road. The seats will be torn and the windows will rattle loose in their frames. The bus will smell. Maybe I will smell, too. Maybe I will be happy to smell. And at nightfall I will get off the bus and there she will be, running toward me with bare feet and windblown hair.

"Mama, Mama!" she will shout. "Mama, is it you?"

"It's me, baby," I will say.

THIS IS NOT THAT STORY

The boy fell from the balcony sometime between 2:00 and 4:00 in the morning. It had already been snowing for several hours, and it continued to snow after he lay on the ground, so that when the dirty white truck rumbled up to the residential quad at 6:15 and three men—the groundskeepers—climbed wearily from the back, armed with shovels, the snow was nearly six inches deep. The old groundskeeper, who was the newest member of the crew, set to work clearing the path that led from the north end of the dorm to the student union, where in just over an hour the dining hall staff would begin serving breakfast. The old groundskeeper was in foul mood; he didn't like his job very much. Leave it to him to pick the worst winter in forty years to become a groundskeeper. His fingers and palms were swollen from shoveling, and his feet were always cold, no matter how many pairs of socks he wore. Every night he sat on the edge of the bathtub and soaked his feet while he read the help wanted ads, looking for something that paid well, that wasn't too noisy, that was—god help him—warm.

The boy was behind a bush. The old groundskeeper probably wouldn't have even seen him had he not stepped to the side, off the path and out of the wind, to light a cigarette. It was the red tail of a shirt that he saw, clotted with snow but bright as a bird. He took a step forward and with the corner of his snow shovel pushed back the bush and saw that the shirt belonged to a boy and that the boy was dead. For a minute he didn't do anything. No, not a minute. Maybe it felt like a minute because he did take a drag on his cigarette—that much he remembered for sure, and he felt guilty for it afterward. He let the bush fall back into place and then took the drag and let it out slow before he reached for his walkie-talkie.

That night his wife made blackberry cobbler. She brought a bowl to him while he sat on the edge of the tub, then slid off her shoes and sat down beside him. She was angry that it was he who had found the boy, that it was not one of the younger men who surely had much less to lose. She feared that seeing the boy would remind her husband of all the other things he had seen and worked so hard to forget, all the other things they'd been running from for so many years.

There's a story there. But this is not that story.

■■■ ■

The night before, around 8:00, a young man signed his name on a form at Big Red's Beer Distributor, promising in writing to return the keg that he was picking up for a party in his apartment that night. The young man was twenty-two, a senior, and the people he'd invited to his party had all been friends since freshman dorm. They were seniors, all of them, and it was early in their last semester of college and so they had net yet reached the cold panic stage—that would blossom with spring—but were in the wonderful stage immediately preceding panic when life after graduation is yet far enough off that it seems any number of breathtaking opportunities might come down the pike before then. The young man had applications being reviewed at several graduate schools—he had just sent them off the week before, so it would be another few weeks at least before he started checking the mail obsessively. This was the time, between possibilities and choices, that he could relax. Though he didn't know it for certain, he suspected that this was the last time that he would secretly believe that anything was possible.

The party was small at first, twelve or fifteen of them. The Girl Who Was Kind Of His Girlfriend arrived around midnight, and the two of them went out back and sat on the stone wall smoking cigarettes in the falling snow. They could have smoked inside, but if they smoked outside then they could use the cold as an excuse to huddle together, and although it was goddamn pathetic (he thought) that after a year of being kind of a couple they still needed this kind of excuse, he was in the process of promising himself that by spring there would be no more kind of about it. He'd gone back and forth on the whole serious relationship thing; they both had, but recently he'd been wondering what purpose was being served—what field exactly they were playing—by only being kind of.

He went into the house to pee. He was drunk by this point and, glancing around on his way to the bathroom, he realized there were people in his home that he did not know. The inevitable tagalongs. The tagalongs of tagalongs. People he didn't know drinking the beer he'd paid for. Well, he'd been a tagalong once, too. Everyone had. You could get pissed about it, spoil your own good time, or you could accept the fact that every social structure in the world relied upon the concept of the tagalong.

After he peed, he went back to the girl. She sat alone on the stone wall, legs drawn to her chest, her chin on her knee, a cigarette snug in her interlaced fingers. There was snow in her hair, and it glistened in the harsh light from the bare bulb over the back door. Later, when he looked back on this night, this was the moment he would remember most clearly. This was the moment he should have said something meaningful, should have said, *"What about next summer? What about next year?"*, or at least told her how beautiful she looked, sitting there on that wall. Instead, he said: "Beer?"

One of the tagalongs in the living room was the boy who fell from the balcony. While investigating his death, authorities discovered he had spent a portion of his evening drinking at the house of the young man. Stymied regarding the best way to portray its grief, the college expelled the young man for providing alcohol to a minor. His plans for graduate school were put on hold. The Girl Who Was Kind Of His Girlfriend never became His Girlfriend. Not because of what happened that night, not directly, but who's to say? It was as if—

But this is not that story.

■■ ■

The chaplain was pretending. Pretending was the only way he could keep from hyperventilating, which he absolutely could not do because there were so many people around—the president, for one, and the dean of students—and frankly how bad would it look if the college chaplain, faced with his first actual on-the-job tragedy, started gasping like a hooked fish? He wasn't pretending that it hadn't happened; that part of it, the death part, he could handle. No, he was simply pretending that the worst was over. He was pretending he had already broken the news to the parents, that he had handled the call with grace and compassion, had been professional yet comforting, and now he was on the other side of that phone call. It was the only way he could breathe—to pretend.

The college had been trying to reach the parents for seven hours and twenty minutes. No one could find them. Not either of them. The father, apparently, was out of town at a conference, but his precise location was unknown—somewhere in Chicago, one of the father's colleagues had told them, but what hotel, what conference exactly, no one seemed sure. The mother, as best as could be figured from a number of phone queries to friends and family, had been running errands all day. No messages had been left at the family home—what would such a message say? How could the caller not give the truth away in tone alone? A command center of sorts had been set up here in the office of the dean of students. Everyone else was milling about, but the chaplain sat at a desk—not even his own, so no opportunity to pretend to do other work—hitting the redial key every three to five minutes.

It wasn't the anticipation of actually delivering the news that was suffocating the chaplain. He just wanted it to be over. He did not like knowing what they didn't know. He had a secret, and once the secret was told, nothing would ever be the same for the people to whom he was going to tell it. The father was at a meeting, the chaplain imagined. At this very moment he was at a meeting and he was not thinking of his son. His son was nestled in the back of his brain, nestled as surely as he had once been nestled in a bed when the father came home late from work and peeked in on him to make sure he was sleeping soundly, to whisper good night. The son was in the bed of the father's brain, tucked away. The mother, the chaplain admitted to himself, could be a different story. The mother was running errands, and this created a variety of terrible possibilities. Perhaps the mother was buying birthday presents for the boy, was at this very moment trying to decide which of two sweaters he would prefer. The boy's file was right in front of the chaplain and the chaplain could see plain as day that the boy was turning nineteen next month. The mother didn't know that her son was not going to turn nineteen. But he, the chaplain, a man who had never spoken to the dead boy, he knew. He, a stranger, knew the most important thing that had ever been known about the boy—that he was no more—and the mother and father who had known the boy intimately, knew nothing. If only he could tell them, then they would know too, and he wouldn't have to carry the weight any longer of him knowing and them not. The rest he could deal with. Tending to grieving students. Speaking to the media. A service, likely outside, during which a tree would be planted, per- haps a plaque dedicated. Future conversations with the parents, meeting them when they came to campus to take the boy's things home. All of this he could handle, could, in fact, excel at. If only he could reach them.

He hit redial again. The machine would pick up after four rings, and he would set the receiver down and—

"Hello?"

His veins turned cold. Wait . . . just wait . . . just . . . never mind. He was happy to keep the secret. Of course he was. He would keep it forever. What had he been thinking? He would—

"Hello?"

But this is not—could not be—that story.

■■■ ■

A little before two that morning the boy was outside looking for a cigarette. The RA, a young woman who faced the world with a desperate, self-effacing cynicism, was standing in the cold, shivering, sucking down a Marlboro Light. She shook one from the pack and extended it to the boy. She had known him for six months. He was among the twenty-four freshmen who were her responsibility, and she had gotten to know him better than most because he was very social and not afraid, like so many of the others, to make friends with the upperclassmen. He was drunk, but not unusually so (she had seen much worse) and thus nothing seemed out of the ordinary until she dropped her finished cigarette onto the fresh snow and saw that the boy wore no shoes.

She nodded to his feet. "Nice. Little cold there?"

The boy shrugged, took another drag off the cigarette.

"Long night?" she asked.

Another shrug. "Hangin' out. You know. Whatever."

"Anywhere fun?"

"Not really."

She was cold, ready to go in and curl up in her afghan. She gave him another cigarette, for the road, and went to bed.

She was the last to see him alive. Because of this, she was forced to recount the meaningless conversation over the cigarette at least a hundred times. On several occasions she was tempted to make parts up, because the conversation (if you could even call it that) had been so utterly dull. She wished that he had said something poignant, or that she had, so that a little solace might be found in his last moments. She was a writer—wanted to be, anyway—and she wanted something writer-ly to have happened there at the end. She wanted to have seen it coming. She wanted to have had a premonition. But all she had was a cigarette. At least she had given him one. At least there was that.

She was not the type to let these things go. It would stay with her forever, his bare feet on the snowy steps outside the dormitory. She would revisit it, seize it with something resembling passion, any time her life veered off course. She would blame herself, exaggerate her role in things, create for herself hundreds of opportunities to save him, opportunities she would have certainly taken advantage of if she'd only been smarter, kinder, a better RA, better friend, better person. Returning to campus for her ten-year reunion, she stepped onto the balcony and felt a grief more acute than she'd felt for her own dead mother.

But this is not that story either.

■■■ ■

Why no shoes? Perhaps the boy had returned from the party, gone into his room and kicked off his battered sneakers, emptied his pockets, checked the answering machine. Possibly he had stepped into the hallway, bound for the bathroom, and inadvertently allowed the door to close and lock behind him, his roommate asleep inside. "Shit," he might have said. It's likely he paused for a moment, considering. There were a dozen rooms he could crash in, friends up and down the hall who would still be awake. But now he wanted a cigarette; if the evening wasn't going to be over, a cigarette was in order. He'd find one to bum, out front, and then figure out where to sleep.

He wasn't in a bad mood, just weary and sobering up, not in the mood to chat. He was glad when the RA gave him an extra smoke and went off to bed, because he wanted to smoke alone. Something nice, really, about smoking alone, enjoying it not because you were being social but because you weren't. But why not just smoke it there, on the steps out front? Maybe he wanted a view of the campus, brilliant and new in the snow. Maybe that was the image of himself he was picturing as the elevator carried him to the fourth floor. A still night, snow falling on his bare feet and head, he alone and above it all.

How did he fall? Everyone has a theory. The railing was high as his chest, so a mere slip on the slick balcony would not have sent him over. Here is what I think: he saw something. Thought he saw something, or someone. Maybe he was waiting for a girl he liked to come home. Maybe he heard voices, friends' voices, from around the corner of the building. Or maybe it wasn't a person at all. Maybe it was a rabbit, or one of the campus cats, trotting down the walk, snow puffing under its light feet. I think he leaned over to get a better look.

But what do I know? Most of this story is mostly made up. Some readers might believe it to be thinly veiled fact, when in truth it is thinly veiled fiction, a fabrication gently draped with the netting of what actually occurred. Half the characters are no more than letters stumbling across my computer screen; the other half have been lovingly adorned with lies and conjecture. "The truth escapes me," people say, though surely we are willing accomplices to its flight. We loosen its chains, leave its cell door slightly ajar, allow ourselves to become distracted as it lumbers off into the waning light. It's easier that way, for then everything and everyone is fair game. Yes, this story's possibilities for the introductory fiction workshop are vast: an exercise in character, in plot, in beginnings, in endings. An exercise in point of view. A story about a college, about a generation, about a culture of excess. A story about the splintering of friendships, about priorities, about the weight of the past, the weight of the future, the weight of the single moment and how it resonates through dorm rooms and classrooms, into bedrooms and waiting rooms, days and months and years away. This story could be all those things, yet it is none of them. So what, then, is the story? Only this:

A boy died.

SWITZERLAND

The suitcase I drag down the attic stairs belonged to my grandmother, so it's one of those old-time deals that already weighs about fifty pounds even without a stitch of clothing in it. I have a photograph of my grandmother with this suitcase. She's standing on the tarmac about to get on an airplane—this was a long time ago, right, when you walked up the stairs onto the plane—that's going to take her to New York and then on to Switzerland, to visit her lifelong pen pal that she started writing to when she was in third grade or something. So she's standing on the windy tarmac, all smiles despite the fact she looks like she's about to be blown off her feet, with this giant suitcase next to her. She's not holding it, 'cause this is the kind of suitcase that even if you just stop for a couple seconds, to have your picture taken, you want to put it down. That's how heavy it is, and when I drag it down the attic stairs it goes *ka-thunk ka-thunk ka-thunk* and I can hear the cats scatter.

The cats. I'll have to leave them. When a woman walks out on her husband she can't take her cats along. How would that look?

"I'm leaving you, but hold on a minute while I wrangle these cats into the car." That's no kind of exit to make. So maybe I'll come back for them. Maybe in a couple months, when I'm settled someplace else, I'll show up in the middle of the day, while he's at work, and I'll use my key (because he wouldn't change the locks . . . it wouldn't even occur to him) and then I'll gather the cats up, one at a time, in a heavy blanket so they don't scratch me to death when they see I'm putting them in the car.

By the time I have the suitcase mostly packed (the essentials— your basic toiletries, the book from the bedside table, underwear and socks and the kind of clothes one would travel in, nothing fancy) it's 4:30 and he'll be rolling in in about fifteen, twenty minutes. By that time I'll have everything straightened and I'll be standing at the door putting on my coat, just slipping my arms into the sleeves as he walks in, so I'm ready to pick up the suitcase and go at just that moment, so I don't have to run back and go to the bathroom or put on my shoes or anything.

His face. It'll go blank first, like somebody's asked him a question in a foreign language. The smile he's worn through the door will sink into his face like cream into coffee. Then, after the blank look, his eyes will narrow, first at the suitcase and then at me. This will only last a moment. The wheels in his head will be turning. At this moment I might feel a little sorry for him. *What did I do to deserve this?* he'll be thinking. I come home from a normal day of work, thinking everything is A-OK, and here's my wife in the front hall with her suitcase packed and her coat on. But he won't say any of this. Instead, he'll swallow really hard, so hard it's like he's trying to get down a pill the size of his fist. Right now he'll be thinking that he can't cry, but he'll want to. He'll be thinking about all the things he should have done differently, how he should have treated me better, how that girl he liked wasn't worth all this.

I wish I had a pen pal in Switzerland. When is it too late to have a lifelong pen pal? Does it count if you start when you're twenty-five? Thirty-five? What if you pretended you were ten? What if you wrote a ten-year-old girl in Switzerland—found her somehow, you know, through the internet or something—and you pretended you were in third grade and your whole life was in front of you and you had all these dreams? Would that be a rotten thing to do? How disappointed would she be when you got off the plane with your big blue suitcase and instead of being ten you were a grown woman? Would she hate you? Or would she just be surprised, and then she'd get over it, and you could still go stay at her Swiss house and eat Swiss-cheese sandwiches and curl up to sleep in a cozy Swiss sleeping bag?

I make the bed. It seems right that I should make the bed, that I should do the dishes, that everything should be just so. I shouldn't leave the house in ruins. It's better if everything is perfect, so he can watch it go to hell once I'm gone. I shake the pillows snug into their pillowcases, imagining how long it will be before the sheets are washed again, how long he'll sleep alone on dirty sheets, how that girl he liked (*It was five years ago, for Chrissakes!* he'll think as he falls asleep on his dirty sheets, as if that makes a difference, as if having cancer for five years is better than having it for one) is with someone else now and now he's got nobody, not her, not me, only two disillusioned old cats. Which I'll be coming back for.

I reach the front hall just in time. I'm opening the closet for my coat when I hear his car outside, the squawk of the brakes, the sigh of the motor, the familiar sounds of his homecoming. I've got my coat on and my keys in my hand, and I pick up the giant suit-case, which must weigh, no joke, fifty pounds. I don't know how she got this thing all the way to Switzerland, my grandmother. I see the doorknob turn and it's in slow-motion—really, it is—like a movie when the murderer figures out you're hiding behind the shower cur-tain and he's coming for you, finally, and you've got nothing but a bottle of shampoo to defend yourself with.

He steps into the hall and takes everything in. His eyes linger on the suitcase, which I'm struggling to keep from dropping. His heart, his pathetic little heart, is crumbling.

"Jesus, Tina," he says. "Not again."

"There's no 'not again' about it," I say. My arm is about to fall off. "This is it."

"Honey." He puts his hand on my cheek. "Honey, really. Aren't you tired of dragging that thing around?

"I love you," he says. "You know that. I *know* you know that."

He says: "Come on. There you go. That's my girl."

He says: "How 'bout we get a pizza?"

END OF DAYS

We had finished up our graduate work some time ago, more than one year, less than five. Now it was May again and a new group was marching off into the world with their theses (they called them books, but we knew better) clutched warmly to their breasts. Some of them had secured jobs and others were pursuing additional meaningless degrees and we mocked and insulted each one of them as Rob's Ford Escort station wagon soared boldly through the night on the back roads of northwest Arkansas on the way to the next battered newspaper tube. This had been Rob's job for three months, his most recent in a string of positions that could have been handled with ease by a crack-smoking seventeen-year-old. Andy and I had joined him on his route this night because, for one, we were all best friends, and for two, we needed a new experience to rehash in the coming months.

"Dibs on this story," Andy said from the backseat. Andy was really a poet (thus, the backseat) but like all poets he had a fat notebook full of story ideas that he was certain he would someday write.

"It's my crap job," Rob said, lighting a cigarette. "So it's my story."

"I hate stories about writers," I said, slugging from the extra-large coffee Andy had brought me from the bagel place where he worked. "You know who never wrote a story about a writer? Chekhov. He didn't—"

"It's not going to be about a writer," Rob said. "It's about a guy who has a retarded brother and the retarded brother wants to help the guy deliver his newspapers, so finally the guy lets him come along and when he gets out of the car to take a piss the retarded brother drives off with the car and all the newspapers."

"Then what?" Andy asked.

"Then nothing," Rob said. "That's the end."

"Did you already write it?" I asked.

"Not yet," he said.

"Good," I said. "Because it sucks."

I took a smoke from his pack of off-brand cigarettes; they were so cheap they didn't even have a name. Back when we were in the program, living large off our stipends, it was Marlboros and Camels all the way. But no more. What money we had went toward five-dollar pitchers at Buzzards, three or four nights a week. When even that was more than we could afford, we hung out in Andy's windowless apartment, watching fifty-cent rentals from Blockbuster. For a while Andy's girlfriend watched with us, but she had been gone a while now, six months, maybe a year.

"Somebody already wrote that story anyway," Andy said. "I read something just like that in a *Best American*."

"You did not," Rob said.

"I did. That whole retarded brother thing. It's like a Denis Johnson or a Rick Bass story or—"

"I hate Rick Bass," I said. "I hate that guy."

"You just hate him because he called you out when he was here," Rob said.

"What did he say again?" Andy asked, leaning into the front seat, like he hadn't heard the story a hundred and eighty-five times before.

Rob grinned. "He told her she was like an ice-skater doing a bunch of fancy jumps and spins in a dark, empty arena."

"I can see where he's coming from," Andy said.

"Shut up," I said. "Anyway, that's not why I hate him. He's just totally overrated."

"At least he's *rated*," Rob said. "You can't be overrated until you're rated, right?"

He slid up next to an old house and stuffed the paper into the tube. It was three in the morning but a couple lights were on inside, and I imagined the guy who lived there sitting at his kitchen table eating a bologna sandwich. There were two cigarettes burning in the ashtray, one his, and one belonging to the woman who'd just gotten up and gone to the bedroom closet to get her beat-up suitcase. It was just like that Carver story. Actually, it was just like a lot of Carver stories.

"Who wrote *The Paperboy*?" Andy asked. "Did Barry Hannah write that?"

"*The Paperboy*'s a kid's book," Rob said. He'd know. His boy was five or six. Or maybe nine. He had a wife, too. She was the long-suffering type, made about a nickel an hour working as a teacher's aide at the elementary school. Back when we all first met she tried to talk to me like we were one and the same, rolled out the whole girl-bonding red carpet. When that didn't work out she thought I might be trying to steal Rob away from her (such a catch, Rob, with his paper route and plotless stories), and after that she just kind of gave up on me altogether. She wasn't alone. At this point, people were lining up outside my door to give up on me. In the gathering crowd I could see parents, siblings, college roommates, disgusted boyfriends. *"Take a number!"* I'd call to them while fetching rejections from my mailbox.

"Nah," Andy said. "There's a story called that, too. Or maybe it's not *The Paperboy*. I know it's *Paper* something."

"*Paper Moon*."

"*The Paper Chase*."

"'The Yellow Wallpaper.'"

"God, I hate that story," I said. "They're always trotting it out. I swear to god it's assigned in every single Western Lit class on campus."

"'Cause it's by a woman," Rob said. "You gotta get your women in, you know. Not a lot of choices."

"Only about a hundred thousand Joyce Carol Oates stories to choose from," Andy said.

"I hate Joyce Carol Oates," I said.

"You gotta have *two* women," Rob said to Andy, ignoring me. "So Oates doesn't seem like your token."

"Alice Walker works," I said. "She's a twofer."

"If only she were blind," Rob said. "Then she'd be a three-fer." He threw his cigarette out the window. "I'm a no-fer," he said. "I'm doomed. I swear to god I'm thinking about changing my middle name to Little Feather. I'm not kidding. It's the only way I'm ever getting a real job."

Rob and Andy often spoke longingly of The Real Job. But they were white guys without books—they didn't think it was even worth the stamps. Not that they'd ever tried. When I pictured myself with The Real Job, the person who was supposedly me was dressed in hip clothes I didn't own and walking professorially across a sunshiny campus, calling clever greetings to eager-faced undergraduates in a voice that was so far from mine it might as well have been dolphin squeaks.

Something briefly flashed ahead of us. It was a deer, standing just off the road, its eyes locked on us as we approached. It watched as we slowly passed, still as a statue, like if it didn't move we wouldn't see it.

"You guys know that poem by Stafford?" Andy asked in a whisper. "That one where the guy hits the deer and then there's a baby deer or something and he kills it?"

"I hate that poem," I said. "It doesn't make any sense."

"How do you know? You ever hit a deer?"

"How much longer?" I asked Rob, readjusting my seat belt so that it wasn't pressing against my bladder. The extra-large coffee had been a serious mistake; for some reason it hadn't occurred to me that there wouldn't be a Taco Bell out here where I could stop to pee.

Rob wasn't paying attention. "What's that story where those guys are deer hunting and one of them shoots the other one?" he asked. "You know what I'm talking about? Who wrote that story?"

"It was in *Best American*," Andy said. "Like maybe two years ago."

"No, this is an old story," Rob said.

"It's Tobias Wolff," I said. "I know that story. I could write that stupid story with my brain tied behind my back."

"So write it," Rob said, flipping on his brights as we turned farther into the dark. "Jeez, write *anything*, why don't you?"

"Hey, now," Andy said, sitting back in his seat. "Easy there, cow-boy."

Rob had broken the Rule of Rules: Don't talk about somebody's work unless that person introduces the topic first. At this stage in our careers (if you could call them that) there was no such thing as friendly encouragement; there was only nail-biting, hair-whitening, heartburn-inducing pressure. Each of us teetered minute by minute on the line between undiscovered genius and complete loser. Why Rob suddenly felt he could nudge me off the line—the late hour? the back road?—I couldn't imagine. But now the gloves were off.

"Don't start with me," I said. "When's the last time you finished a story?"

"Last week," he said.

"Let me rephrase that. When's the last time you *sold* a story? When's the last time you actually—"

"At least I have work out there. At least I'm not—"

"Come on, you guys," Andy said. "We're on an adventure."

We were quiet for a moment. Then Rob said: "An adventure on the rooooooooad to nowhere. Aren't we something special?"

He turned on the radio. Behind a wall of static you could barely make out the thrum of a bass line. It might have been The Who. Rob turned it up and only the static got louder.

The truth, known to no one but these two, was that I hadn't finished a story in over a year. In the program I'd been consistently productive, scored a few decent publications, seemed to everyone (me humbly included) to be headed somewhere. And since then I'd had the ideal job for writing, a sweet gig anyone in my wobbly position would have killed for: I was the monitor at one of the emptiest computer centers on campus. I fixed a few paper jams, rebooted a couple hard drives, but mostly my time was my own. A quiet room with my choice of workstation—I could have written twenty pages a day. But I had a far more important matter to attend to: solitaire. I played so much my vision was blurred by lunchtime; by midafternoon my neck and back were so stiff that I couldn't bend to pick a pencil off the floor. Diamonds and hearts danced behind my eyelids when I went to bed, but the next day I hurried (sometimes *literally* hurried, excited by the possibility of, um, what?) back for more. It was worse than nicotine, worse than beer. Then, at some point, I'd remember with a gust of guilt who I was and what I was supposed to be doing. Every few weeks, say, I'd screw up my courage and begin work on a new story. I'd go like gangbusters for three and one-quarter pages and then, in one terrible instant on the top of page four, I'd see exactly where the whole thing was going and everything that was going to be wrong with it. And so I'd abandon it, hit the solitaire hard, and a few weeks later start the whole process over again.

"I heard Dave Springer got an NEA," Andy said cheerfully.

"Jesus Christ," I said, spinning around to face him. "Why don't you just cut off my fingers and bury me alive? Really, I'd prefer that."

"Sorry," Andy said. "I was just making conversation. He was a nice guy, you know? Remember that party he—"

"He was terrible," I said. "And he was a total kiss-ass."

"Every time a friend succeeds, a little part of me dies," Rob said wistfully.

His statement (which I was about to point out he'd borrowed from Oscar Wilde) was punctuated by the explosion of the rear passenger-side tire. The car veered left, into the absence of oncoming traffic, and Rob pulled it back and rolled slowly to a stop onto the grassy shoulder.

"At least it's not the middle of the night and we're not in the middle of nowhere," Andy said.

Rob snatched the two remaining newspapers and got out of the car, then flung each of them as far as he could into the darkness. "Finished the route," he said. "Now we just got to get home."

"Got a spare?" Andy called from the backseat.

"Not anymore," Rob said. "I used it last month."

"And you didn't replace it?" I asked. I grabbed the cigarettes and followed him out of the car. My bladder was officially full to capacity. "Are there any houses nearby?"

"You want to knock on a stranger's door at three in the morning?" Rob asked. "Every single house within ten miles of here is inhabited by a William Faulkner character. You want to take your chances on which one you get?"

"Caddy smells like trees," Andy said, emerging from the backseat.

"We're gonna have to walk up to the highway," Rob said. "It's probably only three or four miles. Then we'll wave down a truck or something."

"Three or four miles which way?" I asked.

"North," Rob said.

"Which is which way?"

"Up," Andy said. "North is always up."

"That way," Rob said, pointing into the blackness on his left. "We passed a little road just a minute ago. We'll backtrack and then head up that road. It might even go all the way to the highway."

He leaned into the car and cut the lights, and we were plunged into blackness. I couldn't see the car, couldn't see my friends, couldn't see my own feet on the ground below me.

"Flashlight?" Andy asked hopefully.

"Don't think so," Rob said.

For a moment no one said anything, but I could hear them breathing, so I knew I wasn't alone. One time, years ago, we'd been in Buzzards during a summer storm and the lights had cut out. We'd sat there for hours drinking pitchers by the glow of our cigarettes and I remember thinking how lucky I was to have friends to sit with in the dark, to not be in a quiet apartment searching for candles all by myself.

"Turn the headlights on," I said. "We'll be able to see that way for a while. You're gonna have to come back with help anyway, so you can just jump the battery."

He flipped on the lights and we could see again. We started walking down the road the way we'd come.

"*Now* it's a story," Andy said. "You can do the retarded brother thing, but I'm taking this part."

"It'll be boring," I said. "It'll be three idiots walking in the dark talking about stories. You think anybody's going to want to read that?"

"Maybe a bear'll show up and maul one of us," Rob said. He poked me in the arm. "Probably you."

"What's that story where that kid goes camping with his father and the father dies and the kid carries him out of the woods?" Andy asked. "You know what I'm talking about?"

"David Quammen," Rob said.

"Oh, yeah," Andy said. "He came here, like, maybe our second year? He was cool."

"I hate that guy," I said.

Rob laughed. "What'd he say to you? You might want to consider describing what something looks like every once in a while? Just to mix things up?"

"Overrated," I said.

"Would you guys carry me to the highway if I died right now?" Andy asked.

"Not a chance," Rob said.

"What if we both died out here, me and her, and you had to eat one of us to survive? Who would you eat?"

"How many times have we played this game?" I asked. "I mean it, Andy. I swear I've answered this question thirty times."

"Who Would You Eat? never gets old," Andy argued.

"I'd eat whichever one of you had showered most recently," Rob said. "So I'm thinking it would be her."

We reached the turnoff for the road going north. There was still a little light from Rob's car, but up the road it was pitch-black.

"You think we've gone a mile?" I asked, following them into the darkness.

"No way," Rob said. "Half mile, tops."

"I have to pee," I said. "I've had to pee since we got in the car practically."

"Didn't your parents teach you anything?" Andy asked. "You always pee before you get in the car."

"But I didn't have to then," I said. "It's just that, you know, freaking gallon of coffee I just drank." I stumbled on some loose dirt and pitched forward into Andy's back.

"This is no time for flirting," Andy said, steadying me.

"Go on and go," Rob said. "We'll wait on you."

"It's not that easy," I said. "I'm not a guy; I can't just—"

"I know it's not that easy, but it's not brain surgery. I mean surely in your life you've had occasion to—"

"Never," I said. "I mean, latrines, Girl Scout camp, sure. But not actually, you know, *outside* outside."

"Well, then," Rob said. "Looks like today you're doing something new."

"I hate new," I said.

"We can't see anything," Andy said. "If that helps."

"Just keep walking," I said. "Just go on up ahead and I'll catch up."

Their feet scuffed ahead. Andy said: "I showered today. Just so you know." Rob said something back in a low voice. I stepped to the side of the road. No reason, really; it wasn't like anyone was coming, or could see me. But I felt like a bush or tree was necessary . . . at the very least some tall grass. I shuffled forward, waving my arms in front of me until I bumped into some type of shrubbery—it could have been anything: poison ivy, a grove of Venus flytraps. I started to pull down my shorts, but stopped.

It was quiet. I couldn't hear their voices anymore. It had only been a minute, maybe two, but the road—the whole world, from where I stood—was silent. There were no crickets, no rustling leaves, no boys, no stories. It was as dark and still as a grave.

"You guys?"

Nothing. How far ahead could they have gotten? Had it been longer than I thought? Time could go like that, when you weren't paying attention. Maybe I'd shuffled around for five minutes, an hour, half the night. One of my knees buckled slightly, and I struggled to stay upright. I was Neddy Merrill in "The Swimmer," I thought, certain that it had been only a single afternoon when really it had been weeks, months, even years. I was the old woman in "A Worn Path," circling and circling, time compressing and expanding like an accordion. No, worse, I was Connie in "Where Are You Going, Where Have You Been?", a girl alone with nothing to defend herself, nothing between her and a maniac and the soft earth but a flimsy screen door.

"You guys?"

This time it was a whisper, because that was all my airless lungs would support. My friends were gone, had conquered the road in the dark without me, and I was alone. And I had absolutely no idea what to do with myself. All I could do was stand there on my quaking legs, rooted to the spot, unable to move or even formulate a *plan* for moving. I didn't have to pee anymore, but I could not convince my feet to turn back toward the road. My lower lip trembled, and it had been so long since I'd cried that for a moment I didn't even recognize what was happening. I hadn't cried in years, and I was furious with myself for being so weak in the face of solitude. Nothing could break me. Nothing! Except of course the end of "The Dead," which in that moment blew through my bones like a ghost:

The time had come for him to set out on his journey westward.

"BOO!" they shouted, leaping out from the bushes.

"Assholes!" I yelled. "You guys are assholes! I hate you both! You stupid, idiot assholes!"

"Were you scared?" Andy asked.

"Aw, she wasn't scared," Rob said. "Nothing scares her. She was probably happy we were gone."

"Did you pee?"

"No," I said. I was still shaking, and thankful for the dark. "I don't think I have to anymore."

"Sorry if we freaked you out," Andy said.

"We didn't freak her out," Rob said. "Right? Right? You're tough."

I gathered my breath in my lungs. "I've got to get out of here," I said.

"So let's go," Andy said. I felt a hand on my elbow. "Blind leading the blind."

"No," I said. "I mean, for real. I can't do this anymore. I'm telling you, I'm gonna get out of this town."

"Who said that?" Andy asked, his hand falling away.

"Nick Adams," Rob said. "In 'The Killers.'"

"No, I said. "No, it was me."

LIFE OFF MY E

The object in question unspooled from the upstairs bathroom wastebasket as I was going about my Thursday morning duties of emptying the trash. The object in question had been tightly wound in maybe five feet of toilet paper, a tiny, pee-soaked babushka with a plastic grip, a truth-telling window, and a minus-sign face.

"What the *fuck*?" I said. Which is not the way I usually talk, even to myself. That's how surprised I was.

My sister, Lizzie, and I shared a two-story town house in a quiet and well kept "town house community" on the edge of the suburbs. We had finally finally finally finally finally finally realized our dream of being left alone to play Scrabble for the rest of our lives. Not only were there no men in the picture, but there was no chance of men, no dreams of men, no fears of men, hardly even the mention of men, but for the occasional fond recollection of our long-dead father, or the ongoing young Harrison Ford vs. old Harrison Ford argument. We were done with men, and it was officially Scrabble time. But then there was this, this *thing*, in the wastebasket.

That afternoon I played "BABY" off her *B*, with the *Y* on a double letter score. We were sitting at the kitchen table and it was pouring rain outside, a furious, driving rain, a killer of picnics. I watched Lizzie closely, but she didn't miss a beat, just revised the total under my name. She was forty-three years old, so the chances of her being pregnant didn't seem great. But you never know. "Life finds a way," a famous scientist once said, right before the dinosaurs took over all operations at Jurassic Park. Not that I'm comparing my sister to a gender-switching frog. My sister is lovely. She has long jet-black hair and her skin is flawless. Her students regularly fall in love with her. She is five years older than me but looks five years younger.

We had been living together in the town house for about ten months, having both within the space of a year extracted ourselves with the jaws of life from awful marriages, hers an eleven-year boozy carnival ride, mine a six-year house arrest fostering angry, unadoptable dogs. Between us we had exactly zero kids. We also had zero parents and zero other siblings. We had some aunts and uncles and cousins. We each had some good friends. We had steady jobs; we were both spinster teachers now. She taught ninth grade English at a prestigious private school; I taught eleventh grade civics at a sparkling mega high school that looked like a shopping mall. It was mid-June and we had two glorious months of summer in front of us, nonstop Scrabble and Netflix and iced coffee, except for in-service days and workshops and all the other summer hoop jumping required of us to continue raking in those huge paychecks in return for our thirteen-hour days the other ten months of the year.

"So I have to ask," I said, flipping over my newly drawn letters, two *C*s and a *J*. Useless.

She peered at me over her half glasses. They were a recent addition and she looked like a 1950s librarian, which I mentioned whenever I got the chance. She even wore them on a thick silver chain around her neck. "What?"

I chickened out at the last second. "Are you checking your math?"

She leveled the look that made it clear she would not dignify the question with an answer. "One-sixty-four, one-twenty-six."

"Okay," I said. "If you're sure."

She beat me roughly 80 percent of the time—the 20 percent of games I managed to win were due to dumb luck drawing of stellar letter combinations and, very occasionally, if she had a really bad sinus headache. I was no slouch, but it had always been understood by everyone that Lizzie was smarter than me, that Lizzie fell under the category of *creepy smart.* This had never bothered me, even as a child, because I always felt like being *creepy smart* was a burden, a lumpy rucksack of encyclopedias you had to carry around with you wherever you went, something that people would know about you the instant you opened your mouth. I didn't particularly want people knowing anything about me the instant I opened my mouth.

She made the clicking noise with her tongue, which meant she was about to extend her already sizable lead, then neatly laid down "TOMORROW" off my *O*—with a blank for *one of the R's,* but who cared because she got the fifty-point seven-letter bonus.

"Good one," I said. "Nice."

And I meant it. The thing about me that no one ever believes is that I do not have a competitive bone in my body. I honestly do not care if I win, at anything. Lizzie can't understand how a person can *not* be competitive. Once, after I lost twenty-three consecutive games of Othello in a single weekend and remained a good sport about it, Lizzie told me I should apply for disability on the basis of my sustained indifference.

I watched her gleefully update her score and tried to create a list of suspects who could have knocked her up. There was a man two doors down, Kenny. He had recently embraced his bisexuality and now, in his living room, which you could see clearly from the Town House E parking lot, there was a painting of two naked men lounging on chairs in a garden, as naked men often do. There was the PE teacher at her school, whom we had once had dinner with, a man with compact little twelve-year-old muscles and a thin mustache who called everyone by their last name. There was the guy who served us at the coffee place we frequented, the born-again Christian, who always said, "How're the girls doing today?" and gave her (but not me) a little wink. I couldn't imagine it was any of these men, but I couldn't think of any other options.

"Are we playing or not?" Lizzie asked me. "We're not getting any younger."

■■■ ■

Late the next morning I rummaged through the bathroom wastebasket and there was another test, another minus sign. This one was buffeted by at least half a roll of Charmin. Fearing we'd eventually go broke buying toilet paper, I rolled it back up and went downstairs holding the whole thing in my hand. It was about the size of a small rabbit.

She was sitting at the kitchen table drinking coffee and reading the newspaper with her half glasses. She read all the time when we were kids. I mean *all the time*. The only thing she'd give up books for was board games, which is why—at five or six—I'd started playing them in the first place. Otherwise who knows how many years might have passed before she talked to me.

I stood there holding my toilet paper bundle until she looked up at me, and then at the bundle in my hand, and then back at me.

"I know," she said, after a moment. She removed her glasses in the manner of one who is about to be punched in the face. "Okay. I know. Go ahead."

"Go ahead what?"

"Go ahead and tell me. I know it's ridiculous."

Throughout the last couple awful years of our awful marriages we'd played a never-mentioned-but-completely-understood game called I'm Going To Tell You What You Already Know About this Situation, and I'm Going to Pretend I Don't Know that You Already Know It and Just Aren't Acting On It.

I sat down across from her. "Who is it?" I asked.

"A guy from AA," she said.

Of course! Why had I not considered this? She had been sober for over three years, but still made frequent voyages to the top-secret planet of AA, the parallel universe that hovered just outside the existence of the common, non-anonymous majority, the little world within the big world. Sometimes at the coffee shop, or just walking down the street, I tried to catch my sister's eye contact with, her flickering acknowledgment of, other alcoholics. Sometimes I wished I had a secret society for the things that had ailed me in life, perhaps a group for others who had been repeatedly attacked by dogs in their own living rooms.

"What's his name? How old is he?"

She sighed. "Jeremy. Thirty-six."

"Thirty-six! He's younger than me!"

"So what? We're all adults. It's not like he's eighteen or something."

"Does he have a job?"

"He's a magician."

I sat back in the chair. "Maybe you didn't hear me," I said. "I asked if he had *a job*."

"Ha ha." She put down her coffee. "Magician is a job."

"Magician is a job for like two people in all of human history," I said. "Houdini and David Copperfield are the only people ever to put 'magician' under 'occupation' on their tax returns."

"That's so not true," she said. "What about, like, you know, like, what about Karl Wallenda?"

"Karl Wallenda was a tightrope walker," I said. "As you well know."

She was quiet for a moment, and then she grinned. "Do you think he put that on his tax return? God, I hope he did."

I smiled also, picturing the impeccable, precise printing of the tightrope walker on the 1040—tightrope walker—and then realized she was trying to change the subject.

"So are you dating him or what?"

"Just *or what*, I guess. It's not really that serious."

"Serious enough that you're taking a pregnancy test," I said. "Serious enough that—wait, are you *trying* to get pregnant?"

She turned red. Bam—three seconds. The blush rose from her neck and just rolled up her face. It was the perfect blush, humiliating and undeniable, the kind I normally only saw on high school boys.

"Oh my god, you're trying to get pregnant."

"Not *trying* trying," she said. "I'm not guzzling cough syrup to thin out my vaginal mucus or anything."

"What? What? You *are* trying! Only someone trying would know that that was even a thing! Vaginal mucus?"

"I know," she said. "It's stupid. It's . . . never mind. Forget it."

"No," I said, suddenly feeling like the worst sister in the world, dismissing both a love interest and an innocent little baby in the space of thirty seconds. "No, Lizzie. I just mean. No, it's not stupid, it's just a surprise. Are you in love with him or something?"

She shook her head. "I'm not in love with him. He's just nice. He's, you know, really sweet. I just thought . . ."

Her eyes moved to the Scrabble box on the table. Aversion? Or an answer?

"You're sick of playing Scrabble with me?"

"No," she said. "No, I'm not. I just got it into my head that maybe I wasn't done after all."

"I never said you were done," I said. "No one said that. Neither of us is *done*-done."

"You're coming across as pretty done-done," she said.

Which might have been true. When I looked ahead ten, twenty, thirty, forty, fifty years, we were still sitting at this exact table playing Scrabble. Maybe there were people in jet packs zipping by outside. Maybe we had computer chips embedded in our necks. But still: seven letters, one rack, eight triple-word-scores, ten points for the Z. But the picture had lost focus for Lizzie. She had outpaced me, beaten me back into the world. Of course, her marriage had ended almost a year before mine, and she had been by herself, here in this town house without a Scrabble partner, until I had shown up ready to play. And now, game over? So soon?

"But you're not pregnant," I said.

"No, " she said. "Two no's. Pretty definitive. But my period was really late, so, I wanted to double-check. I guess it could be something else."

The "something else" did not need to be named.

"So can I meet him?" I asked.

■■■ ■

He was performing at a community talent show in a small theater on Sunday afternoon. She had been planning to go anyway, so she said I could go along with her.

"We have to sit in the back, though," she said. "He gets nervous if I sit too close."

"So you've done this before."

"We've been together a couple months," she said. "Sometimes when I say I'm at meetings I'm not really at meetings. Sometimes I'm with him. I've seen a few of his shows."

Calling his brief performance a "show" was a bit of a stretch. He was one of about a dozen acts over the course of an endless two hours. Half the acts featured groups of preteen girls singing pop songs and doing cheerleader moves. My favorite act was a husband-and-wife comedy team. They were in their seventies and had a litany of "Kids These Days!" jokes. They had a cassette tape player that the old man held the mic up to at the end of certain jokes and pushed the button for a pretaped rim shot, but at least half the time he pushed the wrong button and instead there would be the whirring of fast-forward. There were about fifty people at the community center, very clearly all related to at least one of the performers.

Jeremy was the second-to-last act, following (in unfortunate planning) another magician who couldn't have been more than fifteen.
Luckily the fifteen-year-old was all about the rings, whereas Jeremy
was a card man.

He was tall and somewhat gangly, with very long and expressive
arms, which were useful for his chosen field. He didn't wear a cape,
like the teenager, which was a relief. He had floppy dark hair and
that prematurely creased face I always associate with years of toil on
the family farm *or* chronic alcoholism. He had a great smile—Lizzie
was right; he was cute—which forced the creases in his face into a
pleasurable arrangement.

His magic was slightly above the birthday party level, consisting
mostly of variations on "Pick a card, any card . . ." He impressed me
once, flinging the deck of cards against the back wall of the stage
and revealing that the sole card stuck on the wall—six of hearts—
was the very card a girl had chosen and shown to the audience moments before. But the applause at the end indicated that he was
neither young nor old enough to really capture the hearts of the
crowd.

Afterward we went out for coffee. The born-again counter
man gave me a little conspiratorial scowl when Jeremy paid for
all three of our coffees; somehow he'd managed to work out that
Jeremy was Lizzie's date and not mine, and now he saw me as a
potential ally. But I was determined to keep an open mind, if for no
other reason than to insist to Lizzie that I had indeed kept an open
mind. We had never been the kind of sisters to bash each other's
boyfriends—to a fault, *perhaps*—but I didn't intend to start looking like a bitter old hag at the precise moment when I was most
feeling like a bitter old hag.

We sat at one of those awkward coffee shop tables that seemed designed for only one person, or two people who didn't mind sitting practically on top of each other. There was only one large table at this coffee shop, and as usual some idiot college student had spread out all over it.

"How long have you been doing magic?" I asked Jeremy, trying to avoid getting my legs tangled in his.

"Most of my life," he said. "But only professionally for the last year. I know—*professionally*." He grinned, cut his eyes at Lizzie. "Believe me, I know how that sounds."

Against my will I liked him. He squeezed my sister's hand on the tiny table and I saw something light up in her eyes, which made me sad and happy at the same moment. Maybe he was magic after all, I thought. Then I nearly threw up in my mouth.

It wasn't as if either one of us had been dying to have kids. We both married late, and both thought it might possibly happen, but even before our marriages turned horrible neither seemed the kind of marriage you wanted to bring children into. For years Lizzie and her carnival-ride (Larry) thought of little but themselves and their own drama. They were both creepy smart, high-functioning alcoholics, a double chronic state that, as Lizzie once described to me, caused them to find each other fascinating almost every night and disgusting almost every morning. As for me, I imagined that my husband's affection for dogs might eventually translate into affection for other vulnerable creatures, but he was so devoted to his cause that the thought of giving it up—giving them up—for something that did not yet exist wasn't even worth discussing. And it was not as if the two could ever coexist in the same house. It was dogs or babies. It could never be dogs *and* babies.

"I was in banking," Jeremy told me. "Before I was in drinking." It was clear he'd used this line before so I did not give him the satisfaction of acknowledging his parallelism with more than a tepid smile.

"He did a lot of work with nonprofits," Lizzie said, lest I think he was simply a shallow, money-grubbing banker.

"I still might get back to it." He looked down at Lizzie; he was probably a foot taller than either of us. "I really might," he said. "I could do both. The magic banker. The banking magician. It's not too late."

"It's never too late," Lizzie agreed.

He nodded. "That's what Carl—" he looked at me "—my sponsor, Carl—that's what he always says. That's his big catchphrase. No such thing as too late."

Somehow the table felt even smaller than when we'd sat down. My resentment for the inconsiderate college student was growing. How could a single person justify hogging an entire four top, while threesomes were clearly killing themselves huddling around a table the size of a large dinner plate?

"I wish I had a sponsor," I said. "I'd like for someone to say encouraging things to me all the time. You guys get all the good stuff. Secret meetings, sponsors . . ."

"I'm not sure I'd say we get *all* the good stuff," Jeremy said. "I've been in jail twice. I don't even have a driver's license anymore."

"She's kidding," Lizzie said. She shot me a look. It was the same look she would sometimes shoot me when we were kids and I'd bother her while she was in the thick of a book. *Can't you see I'm reading?*

"I am; I'm kidding," I said. "I don't need a sponsor. I'm my own sponsor. I'm sponsored by me. When I start feeling bad, I just give me a call, and I say to myself, one day at a time, kiddo. Just take it one day at a time."

"All right," Lizzie said. "You can stop now."

"Or, wait, what's the other thing?" I scooched my chair back from the table, just a tiny bit, undramatically, I thought, but it made a terrible screeching noise. "God grant me the serenity to accept the things I cannot change? Whew—I feel better already. Internal sponsor, coming through in the clutch."

Jeremy looked at me in silence for about five seconds, trying to decide if I was an asshole. Finally, probably because he liked my sister, he gave me the benefit of the doubt.

"You're funny," he said. "Lizzie said you were funny. You guys are both funny."

"Maybe we could be in a talent show," I said.

"I don't think we're that funny," Lizzie said.

■■■ ■

Some of the dogs were very small. Little terriers, weighed no more than eight or ten pounds. He'd come home with the stories about what had happened to them, and I'd be like, who would even *think* of that? He was one of the founders of the first no-kill shelter in our state, but even at the no-kill there were dogs that nothing could be done with, dogs you couldn't in good conscience adopt out to anyone. There had been four of those dogs living with him when we'd met. By the time I left, there were eleven. There were rooms in my house I couldn't enter. We'd both been bitten too many times to count, our arms and legs scarred with wounds he'd stitched up himself because if we went to a hospital then a report would have to be made. "When I said no kill, I meant no kill," he'd said to me on several occasions. And how could you not love a man who cared that much, a man who would stay up all night sitting three feet (no closer, no farther) from a beagle who cried in her sleep, or who cuddled a muzzled greyhound who did not want to bite you, really really did not want to, but would if given the chance?

"Someday they'll find you both dead in the house," Lizzie had said once. (I'm Going to Tell You What You Already Know . . .) "They'll find what's left of you. You wouldn't live with wolves, would you? You wouldn't share your house with tigers?"

And in the end it was true that, all danger aside, all bites forgiven, I no longer loved him but only pitied him, resented him, only felt foolish and cheated for the years I'd spent in that house competing for his affections when it had never even been close. How could I compete with a one-eyed-chow mix who had suffered his whole life, and now, wordless, asked for nothing in return but *just to not be tortured*, nothing in return but simple understanding when he snarled and lunged at the actual hand that was feeding him?

"Maybe tomorrow you could let me get a triple word score," I said to Lizzie, the night after we went out with Jeremy. She had been beating me especially brutally the previous few days, and had just played "LIFE" off my *E* to claim the last triple word score on the board. "Just one, you know? Just maybe you could leave *one* for me tomorrow, if you don't have anything all that great to play on it. What do you think?"

"I thought you didn't care," she said.

"I don't *care*-care," I said. "I just feel like sometimes you could not win by quite *as much*. Are you going to beat Jeremy like this? Because normally people don't really like being *demolished*."

She looked at me over the half glasses. "That's nice that you're so worried about him," she said. "I think he can probably handle it."

"Well you might just want to warn him. That's all I'm saying."

I imagined Jeremy here, at the table with us, the jet packs whizzing by the window, his big stupid octopus magician banker arms reaching out to play some pathetic three-letter word that closed off a whole section of the board, "SIT" off my *I* with his *T* on a double letter score, still thinking he had a chance against her. God, three-person Scrabble. The box said "2–4 players" but that was crap. No serious Scrabble player ever played three-person Scrabble, never mind four. The board was too crowded. There were not enough decent letters to go around.

■■■　■

On Friday Lizzie was at an all-day workshop at her school. I left the house a little before noon to walk to the coffee shop, and saw Jeremy standing in the corner of the parking lot, leaning against a stop sign. I had one moment when I was sure he was actually a creepy stalker murderer, staking out our apartment, but then he saw me and waved his big gangly arm and trotted over.

"Hey," he said. "Can I walk with you for a minute?"

This was when I realized that he had been standing in the parking lot waiting for me to come out. It was muggy and his forehead was slick with sweat. He didn't drive. Where had he come from? How long had he been lurking there?

"Sure," I said.

"Something's happened," he said. He stuffed his hands in his shorts pockets, which stifled his gangliness in a disconcerting way. "Something amazing but I feel really bad about it. My wife and kid are coming back from Ohio."

I only missed one step, but it was a big one, off the curb, and it took me four more steps to not fall down. "I didn't know you had a wife and kid in Ohio," I said, once I had righted myself.

"We've been separated for almost two years. Because of the drinking. Lizzie knew about it. I thought it was all over. But yesterday Julie called and said she wants to give it another go."

I stopped and turned to him. "Does Tina know about the magic?" I whispered.

"What?"

"Nothing. Never mind," I said.

"Listen." He grabbed my arm. It was the kind of grab that was just one degree too rough, the kind of grab that set off warning bells. But maybe he was just frantic. He looked frantic. He looked like he hadn't slept. "They're coming back," he said. "They're getting in the car and driving here. Today. Until I met Lizzie, this was all I ever thought about. This was everything. My girl's seven years old. Next week she's eight."

"That's wonderful," I said. "Tell her I said happy birthday."

He let go of my arm. "Why are you such a bitch to me? You don't even know me."

"Exactly," I said. "Why are you standing on a street corner telling the sister of the girl you're dating that your wife and kid are driving in from Ohio? Why don't you call your sponsor? Why don't you talk to, I don't know, Lizzie? Maybe?"

"I don't know what to say," he said.

"Do you want to give it another go?"

"Of course," he said. "It's my wife and kid."

"And what about Lizzie?"

"I know," he said. His creases creased. He deflated like a big gangly armed parade balloon. "That's the part I feel so bad about. She's a great girl. But, you know. It's my wife and kid."

"And why are you telling me and not her?"

He gathered himself again, looked at me square. "I thought maybe you could tell her for me," he said.

Because men, I thought. Because this was what they did. Because they were capable of love but they were always loving the wrong things: bourbon, Labrador mixes, wife&kid in Ohio. And then they could never get themselves out of anything. There were no tricks for that.

■■■ ■

She was at her workshop until late so it was after ten when we started playing.

"Listen," I said. "I have to tell you something."

"That sounds bad."

"It is. Jeremy told me he's going back to his wife. Or his wife is coming back to him. Wife and kid. From Ohio."

"Wow," she said. "He told you that?"

"Yeah," I said. "He was waiting in the parking lot, all lurky. He didn't want to tell you himself."

"I don't blame him," she said. "I wouldn't want to tell me, either."

She was quiet for a minute. She drew her tiles and began to arrange them on her rack. She didn't seem particularly sad. As a child I always imagined she was too smart to be sad, that the two things did not naturally coexist, that sadness indicated some sort of intel-lectual failure—a lack of grasping the complete situation, perhaps—of which she just wasn't capable. Of course, I grew up and realized this wasn't entirely true, but her sadness still seemed smarter and more respectable—somehow muted, less pathetic—than my own.

"That was his big dream," Lizzie said. "When I first met him, when we were just friends, he told me that was the thing that kept him sober, thinking that might happen."

"Well," I said. "Yeah. I guess it did."

"It must be nice," she said. "To get a prize for not drinking. A reward." She rearranged two letters on her rack. "You know, to *win*. Must be nice."

I tried to think of something funny to say but I couldn't come up with anything. For the first time since I'd moved into the town-house, the days and years ahead seemed like they might be days to be endured instead of relished.

Then she said, "Too bad I don't drink anymore."

She had never said anything like this to me before, not even as a joke. "Do you need to call your sponsor or something?" I asked.

She looked up from her letters. "You are my sponsor," she said. "And I'm yours. We sponsor each other."

"Since when?"

"Since the Carter administration."

"Oh," I said. "I didn't get the memo."

"Well, now you finally know what you've been doing all these years."

It was late. But we had nothing to get up for in the morning. We could play all night if we wanted. There was no one to answer to.

"As your sponsor," I said, "I will now let you beat me at Scrabble."

"That's very big of you," she said.

This is not a story about a new beginning. This is not a story about screwing up your courage and getting back out there. This is just a story about closing the door and playing Scrabble with your sister. At least for a while. At least for the summer.

"Draw your letters already," Lizzie said.

A PROPER BURIAL

It had been three days and the dog was still in the freezer. Simon went down every couple hours to check on her, though what exactly he was checking for he couldn't say. Each time he opened the lid she was still a stiff chocolate Lab with frosted whiskers, stretched the length of the Frigidaire Elite. He'd gaze at her until he felt he was letting too much of the chill escape, and then he'd gently lower the freezer lid and climb the basement steps, the cordless phone moist in his hand.

He'd been trying to reach Rachel since Sunday night. She'd taken Charlie skiing in the Poconos, where her parents had rented a cabin for the week. They'd planned the trip long before the dog had been diagnosed, so of course Simon had initially agreed to it, but when Rachel had come to pick up Charlie on Saturday morning Simon had greeted her grimly at the door, shaking his head.

"This is it," he'd told her. "I swear to god, she's not going to last the day. You can't take him away now."

"We're going, Simon," she'd said. "You've told me eight times she's not going to last the day."

It was true that the dog had been dying for a long time. The vet had said it would probably be only a matter of a few weeks, but it had now been well over two months without a lasting, significant decline. Some days she wouldn't touch her food, but other days she ate with the vigor and single-mindedness of her healthy self. Many evenings she stared dolefully at him with what he was certain were pleading eyes, and he would prepare himself to put her down the following day. But then the next morning she'd explode out the front door and across the lawn after a terrified squirrel. It was like anything else, Simon thought. As it turned out, you could never really tell what the next day of your life would bring. Most of the time even the weathermen were wrong about tomorrow.

But this day, Saturday, was the worst yet. She hadn't eaten since Thursday, had been unsteady on her feet when going outside to pee on the damp leaves that covered the yard. And she hadn't even wagged her tail when the doorbell rang.

"The dog'll probably outlive us all," Rachel said. "I'm not giving up this trip."

So what could he do? He watched his son kiss the dog (on the lips) and the dog thumped her tail once. This was a powerful tail, a tail that had knocked Charlie down at least twice a day when he was a toddler, a tail that had swept glasses and candles off tables, a tail that could sting shins like a belt. One thump was what it had left for Charlie, and one thump was what he got. And then, Sunday afternoon, Simon had been on the couch watching the game and the dog was lying next to the TV. She'd been making sounds, little moans in her sleep, for weeks. Midway through the third quarter he became aware that she was no longer moaning, though he could see the rise and fall of her fur as she lay on her side. He put the game on mute and watched her, rise and fall, rise and fall, no moan, rise and fall, a little flutter of the eyelids, rise and fall. And then: nothing.

He counted to ten, then to twenty, then another slow ten. Still nothing. His eyes moved back to the TV. He watched a down; a penalty flag was thrown. He and Rachel had found the dog tied to a concrete post in the garage of Rachel's apartment building. This was before they were married. He had his own place but spent most of his time at hers. They'd said hello to the dog for three days, coming and going from her car. Then one night he'd gotten up to go to the bathroom, and something (more than a compulsion, but not so fully formed to be an idea) made him go down to the garage and the dog was there, asleep on the concrete, and it was 4:30 in the morning so he knew the dog really belonged to no one, and so he untied her and brought her up to Rachel's apartment and when she woke up she said, "Is there something breathing on my feet?" and they had both laughed about this for years afterward.

The thing was, he'd promised Charlie a funeral. The dog had been a sack of cancer for over two months, time enough for him and Charlie to discuss what would happen. Either Simon would take her to the vet to have her put down, if she seemed in too much pain, or she would die at home. After that, they would bury her in the backyard. Charlie had written out the order of the service one night, while the dog lay at his feet under the kitchen table. The sheet of paper was magneted to the refrigerator.

Opening Remarks	*Simon Winter*
Remembrance	*Charlie Winter*
Guitar Solo	*Charlie Winter*

Burial	*Simon Winter*
Sprinkling of Dirt	*Charlie Winter*
Song	*All*

Charlie had known the dog his whole life. Family and friends had often joked that Charlie was actually Simon and Rachel's second child. A year ago, in the messiest stretch of the divorce, it seemed they might fight over the dog, too. But then Rachel had relented. It was going to be hard enough, she said, shuttling Charlie back and forth every Wednesday; to share custody of the dog was madness. And, Simon knew, there was more than a little guilt involved. She was throwing him out. There was, finally, a limit to the damage you could inflict on a person all at once. Let the man have his dog, for Chrissake. And so he had moved a few miles away to a small house in a cluttered neighborhood, and soon enough the dog learned that this was the way things were going to be, and she stopped straining at the door when Rachel came to pick up Charlie.

Simon descended the stairs again. It was Tuesday night. He'd taken the last two days off work. He could not leave the house with the dog in the freezer. What if he was killed in a car accident? Someone eventually would find the dog in the freezer and think he'd gone insane. Maybe they'd even think he'd killed her, then crashed his car intentionally. Would Rachel believe this? Would Charlie?

The phone rang and he was so startled that he dropped it; it clattered down the stairs and he rushed to retrieve it, then struck his head on the banister so hard that when he straightened up for a moment he thought he was going to faint.

"Hello?"

"It's me," she said. "I know I said we'd call. I'm sorry. There's no access at this place and—"

"She's dead," he said. "I've been trying to call you since Sunday. She died. She's dead."

"Oh, my sweet baby," she said, and he knew that if he'd been able to tell her in person that they would have embraced now, that it would have been *the thing* that finally overshadowed everything else and he would have gotten at least one goddamn decent moment out of all this. But like this, three hundred miles away, he gained nothing from her sadness. Her grief was as worthless as his own.

"Do you want me to tell him?" she asked.

"I'm not going to fight you for it," he said.

"That's not what I meant," she said. "I just meant—"

"When can you leave?" he asked. "Can you get home tonight?"

There was a pause. Then: "What?"

"Can you leave tonight? If it has to be the morning it—"

"Why would we leave?" she asked.

"We have to have a funeral," he said. He crossed the basement to the freezer. "I promised him we could have a funeral."

"You can have one when we get back," she said. "It doesn't matter when it is, does it?"

"I have to bury the dog," he said. "I can't just—"

"Wait a minute," she said. "You haven't buried the dog? When did she die?"

"Sunday," he said. "Before dinner."

"Well, where is she? At the vet?"

He opened the lid and looked inside. "She's in the freezer."

"The freezer. Our freezer?

"*My* freezer. You got the fridge; I got the—"

"The dog is in the freezer?"

"I told you, we have to have a funeral. He and I have—"

"Stop, Simon. Listen to me. Bury the dog today and then you can have the funeral when we get back."

"There is an order of service," he said. His ear hurt, and he realized he was grinding the phone into the side of his head. He switched to the other ear. "He had a plan and the burial is part of it and I'm not going to take this from him."

"Don't pretend this is about him," she said. "I think he'll be willing to change the order of service, just maybe, so that the dog doesn't have to lie in state in your basement." There was a pause. Then she said, "Is she frozen? Is there, like, frost on her and stuff?"

"Her tail's like a stick," he said.

"Jesus, Simon," she said, tenderly, though he thought the tenderness was more for the dog than for him. "Bury her, please."

"Bring him home," he said.

"We'll be back Sunday," she said. "My parents have waited a long time for this trip with him. I'm not going to just sweep him away because you're too messed up to bury your dog."

"It's his dog, too," he said. "He wants to give her a proper burial."

"He's eight," she said. "I think a memorial service will suffice."

"Put him on the phone," he said.

"No," she said. "Not when you're like this."

"Put him on the fucking phone or I'll call the lawyer."

"Simon," she said. "Jesus, Simon, he's not even with me, okay? He's out with my dad. Will you call somebody, please? Will you call Jerry or your sister or somebody? You need somebody to—"

He touched the dog's icy stomach. "You remember that time in the park when she picked up that turtle? You remember—"

"No," she said. "I'm not doing this. We'll call you tomorrow, okay? Get yourself together and we'll call you tomorrow and you can talk to him. And we'll be home in a few days. I have to charge my phone, okay? I have like one bar left and I have to stand in the middle of this town to get anything. I swear to god I'm standing in the middle of an intersection right now."

"Sure," he said. "I understand. You only have one bar left. You've only had one bar left for about the last five years."

"Good-bye, Simon," she said.

And then, abruptly, she was no longer beside him in the basement but instead standing in the middle of a snowy intersection in a little town in Pennsylvania. He pushed the off button on the phone, looked down at the dog. Once, when the dog had stepped on a nail and gotten six stitches in her paw, Rachel had made a bed on the living room floor and they'd all spent the night huddled together like a litter of puppies. He imagined her now, at the snowy intersection, blowing into her hands. Her knuckles were bright red. He imagined holding her cold hands, squeezing them between his own, until her fingers broke.

■■■ ■

He had some drinks. He could have called someone. He could have called his friend Jerry and Jerry would have come over and had drinks with him and talked trash with him about Rachel and told sweet stories about the dog, but frankly he was not interested in anyone intruding upon his misery. After Rachel had thrown him out his sister had come over every day for two weeks. She'd cooked for him and done his laundry and said lots of encouraging things and finally he'd asked her to please stop being so supportive and go home.

Now it had been almost a year since the split and his sister and some of his friends were trying to fix him up. His sister had told him he was a hot property, that for every date-able guy in his midthirties there were ten datable girls. He didn't doubt this was true. But he didn't want to date anyone. Dating was awful, and he resented he'd been put in the position to endure it again. He was supposed to be finished with that part of his life. He'd done it already, had succeeded at it, found the woman he wanted to marry, and that was supposed to be that.

That she had someone else was what he'd thought, of course, when she'd sent Charlie to her parents a year ago and said they had to have a serious talk. There was someone else—it hit him with complete clarity and certainty—and as he sat down at the dining room table across from her he could picture the guy perfectly and instead of anger he felt sheer panic, like he was blindfolded and standing on the edge of a building. And then she had said this thing:

"I don't know where I'm supposed to end up, but I know it's not with you."

And then she had apologized! "I'm sorry, Simon, I got the sugar-free ice cream; I'm sorry, Simon, I forgot to take the dog out; I'm sorry, Simon, I don't know where I'm supposed to end up, but I know it's not with you."

For a moment after her apology he ceased to be a man and existed merely as a cliché. The wind was knocked out of him; his mouth fell open; his vision blurred. His actually felt a stabbing pain in his heart, as if she'd gone after him with a couple of her knitting needles. Who knew it could really happen like that, just like on TV? All the obligatory crap, it all came down. The weeks that followed proceeded like an endless colonoscopy, one indignity after the next. And now his dog was dead. So it was only right that he have a few drinks.

■■■ ■

At 3:15 the next afternoon the doorbell rang. It was Lucy, the high school student who gave Charlie guitar lessons. Lucy kept her hair in a long braid and wore faded flowery skirts thay swayed at her ankles. She lived down the street and came every Wednesday after school to work with Charlie on songs like "House of the Rising Sun" and "Five Hundred Miles." Simon had forgotten to tell her not to come this week; when he saw her shivering at the door his heart briefly lifted, so he invited her in and got her a cup of tea and sat down with her in the living room. When she asked after the dog, who usually greeted her with at least a healthy wag, he told her she was in the backyard.

"Is Charlie out there?" she asked. She propped her guitar against the arm of the couch.

"No," he said. "He's not home yet."

"That's weird," she said. "But sometimes the buses run late."

"Yes," he said, with an air of finality he hadn't intended. The room fell silent, no boy's footsteps or dog's pants to fill the space. She sipped carefully at her tea. Unable to think of anything else to talk about, he added, "Do you ride the bus?"

"Not anymore," she said. "My boyfriend has a car. But I used to. Do you remember when the guy was run over in the school parking lot? That was *my* bus that did it."

"Really?" he said, though he had no memory of the event.

"He died like *that*," she said, snapping her fingers in an approximation of instant death. "It was the last day of school. Someone dared him to lie under the tire, and he did it because he didn't think the bus driver was even on the bus, but it turned out the driver was just bent over picking a candy wrapper off the floor, and then the driver sat up and pulled forward."

"Jesus," he said.

"Yeah," she said. "I didn't know him. He wasn't in my grade or anything. But it was still horrible." She leaned forward and lowered her voice. "You want to hear the really freaky part?"

"It gets freakier?"

She nodded. "They said they got a new bus, over the summer, because a bunch of parents called and said they shouldn't make the kids ride a bus that killed somebody. So on the first day of school the next year we had a shiny new bus with a new number. But then I sat down in my seat, the third from the back, where I'd always sat since third grade, and ever since third grade there'd been this little flap in the seat in front of me where I could stick my gum in the morning and pick it up again in the afternoon, and I thought now I'd have to swallow my gum because I wouldn't have the flap anymore. But guess what?"

"What," he said.

"The flap was still there. Even my gum was still there, inside it; I never picked it up the afternoon of the accident. It was gray. The gum, I mean."

"It was the same bus," Simon said.

"Exactly," she said. "They just painted it and gave it a new number. I wrote a song about it: 'You Can't Just Change the Number.' You wanna hear it?"

"Wow," he said. "Absolutely."

She reached for her guitar, pulled it into her lap. "It's kind of a metaphor," she explained.

"Cool," he said, sitting forward in his chair.

She strummed one note, a particularly sad one, Simon thought, which was odd because it seemed like a note should not be able to be sad on its own but only in its relationship to others. But then something stopped her—he could see it come across her face, the realization that something in the house was off, even corrupt—and she lay her hand over the strings to silence them.

"Aren't you worried about Charlie?" she asked. "He's really late."

"Charlie's on vacation with his mother," he said. "And the dog's not in the backyard. The dog's dead. She died on Sunday."

"Oh no," Lucy said. "Oh, Mr. Winter, I'm sorry. She was a sweet dog."

"She never tore anything up," he said. "Not one shoe. Not one piece of mail. And she'd even let you give her a bath, you know? She'd just stand there while you held the hose on her."

"I know," Lucy said. She stood up, holding her guitar in front of her. She looked slightly nervous, Simon thought. Well, he reasoned, he'd outright lied to her; maybe she had a right to be nervous. "Listen, if Charlie's not here, I think I should probably get going," she said.

"You want to stay for dinner?"

"It's quarter to four," she said.

"We could have an early dinner," he said. "I could put some burgers on the grill."

"Mr. Winter, it's like forty degrees outsi—"

"Your boyfriend could come," he said. "And your parents. Are they home? I could call them."

He had an image now of a yard full of neighbors, though except

for Lucy he didn't know a single one of them by name. In the picture in his mind he was standing at the grill wearing an apron that
said "Top Chef." He was surrounded by a crowd of trim people with
gleaming white teeth. They were all laughing and drinking beer; an
attractive black man slapped him jovially on the back. The scenario
was so familiar that for a moment he thought this had once been his
life, a life snatched from him by Rachel. Then he realized he'd seen it
all recently in a TV commercial.

"Never mind," he told Lucy. He stood and walked with her to
the front hall.

"Did you have her cremated?" Lucy asked. "When my dog Wil-
loughby died, we had her cremated and then we sprinkled her ashes
at every house on the street. All the places she used to pee."

"She's in the freezer," Simon said, opening the door for her. He
was suddenly very tired from all the company at the pretend barbecue.

"What freezer?" she said. "You just have that dorm fridge."

"I got a full-size freezer in the divorce," he said. "It's in the basement. I had some Bomb Pops in there but I threw them away."

Lucy's eyes widened. "She's really in the freezer?"

"Yep," he said.

"Can I see her?"

"No," he said. "You were right—you should go." He didn't want
anyone to see the dog. If someone else saw her it would be real, ir-
refutable, kaput. As long as he was the only witness there was a slim
chance it wasn't true, because he was half out of his mind anyway,
so who was to say the dog wasn't at the kennel, or down at the park
with a soggy tennis ball in her mouth, just waiting for someone to
wing it across the sky?

■■■ ■

At 10:30 he put on his coat and left the house for his nightly dog walk. He nearly carried the leash with him, imagined dragging it limply behind him, but to do so seemed showboat-y pathetic, something a sad sack would do in a silent movie. Every night that Charlie wasn't staying with him, he and the dog had walked the same walk, left at the end of the driveway, past the neighbors he almost never saw, past the house with the old black Lab who watched from the window but never barked, past the house with a half dozen rusty bicycles in the yard, past the house where Lucy lived with her parents, on down the street to the stop sign, a left turn, and past the house where the young man sat smoking on the porch, past the house with the alarmed beagle, past the house where the windows were always dark, past the house with the Redskins flag fluttering from a pole, past the house where the kids were always screaming. He stopped now and listened to them, their voices genderless, the kids—at least three of them, maybe four—preteens and furious.

He saw his life taking shape before him, falling in line like so many houses down this street, saw Charlie returning home from the Poconos and almost immediately asking for the car keys, then departing for college, then at the altar, then an infant sleeping on his chest. He should have slowed things down somehow, back when he had everything, should have dug his feet into the ground four or five years ago and refused to let the earth spin those seasons away.

The next house was the one with the fat gray cat who always sat on a chair on the porch, who raised its head when he passed with the dog and then, seeing nothing of interest, set it down again upon its paws. Simon had never seen another soul on the porch, never seen anyone petting the cat, though it was fat and well groomed and obviously lived in this house. Who were these people? he wondered. Were their lives so full they couldn't take five lousy minutes out of the evening to spend with their cat?

He stopped in front of the house. It was cold, and he could see tiny cat breaths billowing from the cat's mouth. He glanced up and down the street and saw no one. Quickly he climbed the six steps to the porch and scooped the cat, mid-billow, into his arms. He cleared all six stairs in a leap, stumbled two steps on the sidewalk, then dashed down the street and around the corner, already fumbling for his keys with his free hand. When he reached his house he opened the door and then quickly shut it behind him. Still holding the cat, he pressed his eye to the peephole. The street was vacant. No one had seen him. Breathing heavily, he stepped away from the door and gently set the cat on the floor. The cat flopped lazily onto its side, licked the bottom of its paw, then looked up at him with almost no interest whatsoever.

He knelt down and stroked the cat, and the cat raised its back into his head and flicked his tail. It didn't seem concerned at all to be in a new place. Simon had never had a cat, but he knew what people said about them, that they were aloof and superior and had few loyalties. It had probably already forgotten its old home, Simon thought; the memory of the rotten family who'd kept it outside day and night was at this moment swiftly evaporating within its miniature brain. But then the cat stood up and walked over to the door and batted its paw in the direction of the doorknob.

"Mrow," the cat said.

"No, no, no," Simon said, shaking his head. He picked up the cat and turned it so they were face to face. "This is your home now. On Saturday Charlie'll be here. He and I'll take good care of you. We won't leave you sitting in the cold all night long."

He carried the cat into the bedroom and set him on the end of the bed. The cat again flopped onto its side and unenthusiastically licked its paws while Simon changed into his pajamas and then stepped into the bathroom to brush his teeth. When he came out the cat was gone. He found it back in the front hall, lifting its paw and talking to the door.

"Mrow," it said.

"No, no, no," Simon said. He picked up the cat again. "Listen," he said. "Tomorrow I'll get you some canned food. Top of the line, okay? The one on TV where the cat eats out of the crystal bowl. And I'll get you a litter box and a new collar and some little mouse toys. Okay? Okay?"

He carried the cat into the bedroom and laid down on the bed with the cat resting on his stomach. He stroked the cat and the cat was content, for a minute or two, and then as Simon was drifting off he heard the thump of its feet on the floor.

"Fine," he said, swinging out of bed, suddenly wide-awake and furious. "If that's the way you want it."

He stomped out to the front hall and yanked opened the door. The cat walked outside and flopped down on the front walk. It hadn't wanted to leave, Simon realized. It had just wanted to go outside. Simon looked at the clock. It was a little after midnight, a few minutes into Thursday. He couldn't wait until Sunday to bury the dog. Rachel was right: he was losing his mind. She hadn't said it in so many words, but it was surely what she'd been thinking standing there with her one paltry bar, and she was right. He had a frozen dog in his basement and he'd just stolen a cat off somebody's porch, which was probably a felony. Who knew what he'd do next?

He was going to have to bury the dog, and he was going to have to do it now.

It had been easy, getting her down the stairs and into the freezer, because she'd still been warm and pliable and had relaxed into his cradled arms as if she were a sleeping child. But now she was cold and hard and he understood the term "deadweight." At first he tried balancing her across his arms, but she kept slipping off to one side, so then he tried putting her over his shoulder, but she slid off and made a sickening cracking noise when she hit the basement floor, so he decided he'd have to drag her up the stairs. He tried to do it gently, pulled her backward by the shoulders. When he reached the kitchen he picked her up around the middle, pretending she was a statue instead of a real dog, and pushed out the back door into the yard. He lay her under the maple tree, the place he and Charlie had chosen for the grave, and then went to the garage to find the shovel.

But of course there was no shovel. The shovel he had so clearly pictured hanging on a peg in the garage was actually hanging on a peg in another garage, three miles away, in a home that was no longer his. So she'd taken his shovel, too. Yes, it was true, he'd told her he didn't want it, couldn't remember ever using it, but she'd been awfully quick to accept the shovel . . . and the spade, and the hedge clippers, and the weed whacker, and all those other gleaming things they'd bought at Home Depot but never used. He poked around the garage and found some of Charlie's old sand toys. It was worth a try, he thought.

He went back out to the yard and got down on his knees on the cold ground, stabbed at it with a blue plastic shovel, which immediately snapped in two and sliced his hand open as it broke. He swore, pressed the wound to his pajama pants, then grabbed a bright-yellow, claw-like implement, which managed three decent scratches in the dirt before it, too, snapped in his grasp. He went through another half dozen toys and, by the time they all lay scattered and broken around him, had made a shallow trench possibly just large enough to bury a goldfish.

He went back into the house, muddied and spattered with his own blood, to find something else to dig with. In the kitchen he seized upon a trio of possibilities from the items he'd won from the marriage: a spatula, a meat fork, and an ice cream scoop.

He returned to the shallow trench. It was cold out, but in minutes he'd worked up a sweat and he peeled his shirt off so that he was wearing only his pajama pants and his slippers, which were quickly becoming caked with dirt. The spatula was useless for anything but scraping, but the combination of the meat fork and the ice cream scoop showed promise. He could loosen the soil by stabbing with the meat fork, then shovel it out with the ice cream scoop. He paused for a minute to wipe sweat from his eyes and saw that the cat had come around the corner of the house and was standing at the edge of the patio watching, looking from person to dog and back again, trying, Simon imagined, to decide if either of them (scoop-handed man, lying-down dog) posed any kind of threat.

He went back to work, digging with both the scoop and his bare hand. He guessed he'd made about enough progress to bury a guinea pig. At this rate it would take him until morning to dig the grave, and the dog was de-frosting by the minute. When the sun came up, things would likely get ugly in a hurry.

A wave of light burst across the yard.

"Everything okay here?"

Simon stood and turned and blinked into the blinding light. He could make out the dim outline of a figure behind it. It was a cop, he thought. Of course, a neighbor had seen him out here, digging like a maniac, blood on his shirt, and called 911. Simon couldn't see much in the glare, but for all he knew there was a gun leveled at him, the safety unlocked, the trigger fingered. For all he knew, one move and he was dead, fallen beside his thawing dog. Fitting, yes, that it would come to this, that Rachel would get another call on her failing phone, this one to inform her that he himself was dead, was lying in a freezer that was not a Frigidaire Elite. But then, as the possibility of this last drama was at its ripest, he imagined Charlie without a father *and* without a dog. The drama deflated before his eyes. There was, finally, a limit to the damage you could inflict on a person all at once.

"It's Ted Oliver, from down the street," the voice behind the flashlight said. "Lucy's dad. Are you all right?"

"My dog died," Simon said.

"That's what she told me. I was bringing the trash around and heard you down here. Thought I'd come see what you were up to."

The beam of light dipped to the ground around his feet, where Charlie's sand toys and the muddy utensils lay.

"You're digging with a fork?" Ted Oliver asked.

"I don't have a shovel," Simon said. "My ex-wife got it."

Now Ted clicked off the light and crossed the yard to the tree. He was a thin man with round glasses and a neatly trimmed beard.

"I've got one of those," he said.

"A shovel?"

"No. Well, yes, that too." He smiled and adjusted his glasses. "An ex-wife was what I meant. Lucy's mother. Left in the middle of the night when Lucy was three years old. Took the car and the credit card, didn't even leave a note. She was screwed six ways to Sunday but I missed her so much it nearly killed me." Now he nodded to the dog. "Old age?"

"Cancer," Simon said.

"Want some help?" Ted asked. "I'll grab that shovel. I suspect we could make quick work of it together."

Simon considered. "Okay," he said finally. "I mean, if you want."

"Nobody *wants* to bury a dog," Ted said. He knelt down beside her and lay his hand gently on her head. "She seemed like a good one," he said. "I'd see you walking. She matched you stride for stride."

Simon looked at the dog. Her fur was wet now, slick like after a bath. She looked like herself again, and he was sorry he'd kept her down there so long, becoming all the things she wasn't—cold and hard, freakish, a memory of another life, a bad joke. She was just a dog, a friendly brown dog, whom he'd untied from a post in the middle of the night and taken in, and loved.

INDULGENCE

My mother was thrilled to be dying of brain cancer after a lifetime of smoking. She had dodged the bullet of lung cancer after all, she triumphantly announced to me on the phone that summer afternoon. All those years my brothers and I had hassled her, lectured her, begged her, berated her ("Don't you want to see your grandchildren graduate from college?")—and for what? Her lungs were fine! She'd finally quit two years before, after a bitter and tumultuous relationship with patches and gum and hypnosis and electric cigarettes, but look! There'd been no need! The long-dreaded cancer had found some other place to roost.

"What do you want me to do?" I asked her. "Throw a party?" I was trembling from the inside out—my mother was *dying*—and furious at her for reporting her diagnosis so flippantly, as if I, too, would be so thoroughly amused by the irony that the news would just roll right off me. I looked out the kitchen window and saw my children in the backyard, their half-naked bodies slick from the sprinkler, their hair nearly sparkling in the sunlight. It was a suffocating Midwestern Saturday smack in the middle of July. My son was rolling up my daughter in a badminton net.

"I would love a party!" she said. "Just the two of us. Leave Kevin with the kids, and we'll send your father away and *indulge* for a few days. Can you?"

"I don't know if I can think of it as a party," I said.

"You can," she said. "For me, you can. I'm like one of those dying children who gets to make a last wish. What are they called?"

"Dying children," I said.

"See?" she said. "You *are* ready for a party. Can you come?"

I could. I did. I went the next day. Not quite the next day. Arrangements had to be made: work, children, husband—*the full catastrophe*, as Anthony Quinn famously said in my father's famously favorite movie. I went the next weekend. I got off the plane on a Friday morning with four cartons of cigarettes in my carry-on: two Carltons, her old brand, and two Winston Lights, the brand I had appropriated from my oldest brother when I was a sixteen-year-old cripple.

"Oh, honey," she said breathlessly, when I opened my carry-on to reveal the precious cargo. "Oh, honey. Really?" She had to set her hand on a chair back to steady herself, and she wasn't being funny or dramatic. The last time she'd looked at me that way was the first time she saw me pregnant.

"The cigarettes are innocent," I said. "We must celebrate the cigarettes."

■■■ ■

My father knew when he wasn't wanted. He hugged me in the driveway and went to visit my nearest brother for the weekend. My father had never been a smoker. He had no dog in this race. He was just a regular guy, a skinny engineer who could kick your ass at Ping-Pong and whose wife was dying of brain cancer. Six to eight months, the oncologist had told them, time enough for her to have a few days alone with her only daughter.

"You look great," I said, after I'd dumped my stuff in my old bedroom and come out to the living room. I wasn't lying; she didn't look like a person *suffering* from anything. She was a tallish woman with still exquisite posture. Her black hair had never grayed and now never would. She wore solid-colored cardigan sweaters nearly every day, even in the summer, because air-conditioning always made the hair on her arms stand up. She looked essentially the same as she had the last time I'd seen her, when they'd come west at Christmastime and shared my son's bunk bed, my father on the top bunk because my mother "didn't like heights." ("It's not really a *height*, Nana," my son had told her, and they'd laughed about it all week.)

"I feel fine," she said. "If they hadn't told me I was dying, I'd never know it."

She'd already broken into a carton of Carltons, in exactly the way a dog would break into a package of bacon thoughtlessly left on a coffee table. Pieces of the box were strewn across the room. Now she flicked the lighter and took a drag so deep that I thought the smoke might seep from the tips of her shoes. "Oh my god," she said. "Oh my god, Christine, thank you."

I sat down on the couch and opened my own carton, removed a pack. I remembered once, on a Christmas Eve many years before, my father had left the festivities to buy my mother two cartons of cigarettes, and when he got home he commented on the irony that the cigarettes were more expensive than any of the Christmas presents he'd gotten her. *And more beloved,* we'd all thought, though no one said it.

"Are you in pain?" I asked her.

"Very little," she said. She ashed her cigarette. Ashtrays had already sprung up all over the living room; apparently when they'd been removed, they hadn't gone far. "Even less right now."

I smacked my pack of cigarettes on my open hand until my palm stung, then undressed the cellophane and—with a quick strike to the index finger—knocked the first cigarette loose. I withdrew it gently from the pack and slowly ran it under my nose. It had been a dozen years since I'd had a cigarette—I'd smoked through grad school, simultaneously earning a master's in architecture and a thin, musical wheeze—and twenty years since that wonderful winter and spring I'd spent chain smoking with my mother. The tobacco was sweet and made my nostrils tingle.

"First this," my mother said, sitting down across from me and pushing a stack of papers across the coffee table.

"What is it?"

"For pulling the plug," she said. "I don't think your father has the stomach for it. And your wishy-washy brothers won't—"

"I just got here," I said. "I haven't even taken my shoes off."

"I'm getting my affairs in order," she said. "Haven't you seen any movies about people dying? The plot demands it."

"Okay, then," I said. "But only because the plot demands it." I signed the paper as the *X* instructed. It occurred to me after I set the pen down that I should have actually read the document. It could have demanded anything. I could have just agreed to give her my own brain. I could have agreed to sprinkle her ashes on my cereal. But I was anxious to get to my cigarette.

"No extreme measures," she said. "When you think I'm gone, *pfffft*"—the cigarette like a blade across her neck—"I'm gone."

I rubbed my thumb on the lighter before igniting it. "If you just drift off on the couch—?"

"When you think I'm gone," she said, "I'm gone."

I touched the quivering flame to my cigarette, she turned on the television, and we settled in. After a moment she let out a long, satisfied sigh.

"What?" I said.

"You're just what the doctor ordered," she said, not turning from the TV. She ground out her first cigarette and reached for another.

■■■ ■

A week after my sixteenth birthday, I was hit by a car and fractured my spine in three places. An old man veered off the road and struck me while I walked to the bus stop on a bone-chilling Tuesday morning. I never saw it coming. One minute I was reciting French verb tenses, and then I was in the air, twisting, twisted, flying on the edges of a joyful memory of my father flinging me into a swimming pool. I landed with a jolt that went from my toes to my teeth. The concrete sidewalk was bitter cold, and I was alone, and I looked into the bright blue sky and believed I was dead, until the old man was beside me in a panic, shouting at me to stand up, and when he took my arm and pulled, I felt things inside me fall apart, bones ripped from muscle torn from skin, and I lost consciousness.

For a time, a very short time, only a couple of days really, there was some terror about whether I'd walk again, but the surgery to repair my spine went off without a hitch, and after two weeks in the hospital, I was sent home to recuperate, which meant sleeping in long after my father and brothers had left the house, glancing at the schoolwork that had been packaged up for me, shuffling to the car, sweating through a couple of hours of grueling physical therapy, shuffling back to the car, and then returning to the cocoon of my living room, my mother, and my pain medication.

My mother was, had always been, a stay-at-home mom. She had raised my brothers and then me, excelled at room mothering, delivered Meals on Wheels, knitted hats and mittens for the poor, given back to the world in all the ways that mattered. But she was home, or *could* be home, and so during my recovery we spent every day together, playing cards and watching television, which was pretty much all I was good for during that first month after the hospital, and furthermore all I especially *cared* to be good for.

It was February, and O. J. Simpson was on trial on seven different channels, so every afternoon we'd watch the trial and play lazy hands of gin rummy, and when I started smoking my brother's cigarettes and drinking my mother's Maxwell House coffee, she didn't say a word, because my back was broken, and I had been knocked out of my shoes by a 1987 Buick while walking on the sidewalk—the sidewalk!—and every time I stepped outside my house, even if only for a short, therapeutic walk to retrieve the mail from the box at the end of the driveway, I was jittery as a squirrel.

■■■ ■

"I've missed cigarettes," I said that first night. We'd each blown through an entire pack over the course of the afternoon, then ordered Chinese takeout late in the evening when we realized we'd have to put something else in our mouths. Now we were in the kitchen schlepping the food onto plates and sneaking in one more smoke before we had to take a dinner break.

"I used to miss cigarettes *between* cigarettes," my mother said. She gazed wistfully at the lo mein. "After I quit, I thought about them all the time. I didn't go an hour without thinking of them—maybe I didn't go ten minutes. I missed them more than I ever missed any person." She didn't say anything for a moment. Then she looked up from the lo mein and said: "Feel free to leave that out of the obituary."

The smoke hung thickly in the kitchen, but it was a pleasant thickness, like being wrapped in an old, heavy blanket. If it had been only her smoking, I probably would have found it unbearable, vile. But it's a fact of smoking that the smoke you contribute never seems as suffocating or smells as bad as the smoke of others.

The kitchen was the smallest room in the house, which had rarely presented a problem in our family. For all her homemaker qualities, my mother had never placed a premium on cooking; the food of my childhood had been simple, with meals often eaten on the run. My brothers and I always had somewhere to be. We ate grilled cheese and soup. We ate tuna fish sandwiches. Sometimes we had spaghetti, but we were forever reheating.

"Hey, Mom," I said. "I left that pan on the burner."

She glanced at the stove. "What pan?"

"The pan with the vegetable soup. You know, that time. It wasn't Bryce. I turned it on, and then I went to take a shower, and I forgot about it and went to bed."

"I know," she said. "I knew then and I told you I knew."

"Yeah, but now I'm telling *you*. I'm admitting it." I carried my plate to the kitchen table, took a quick last drag, then crushed out my cigarette and picked up my fork. "I'm sorry I lied. And I'm sorry I blamed it on Bryce. It was a crappy thing to do."

"It was twenty years ago," she said. "No one died. It was one ruined pan."

"But I—"

"You want me to forgive you?" she asked. "All right, there, I forgive you." She threw her cigarette in the sink. "Now can I eat?"

■■■ ■

It was not, at sixteen, that I thought smoking was cool. Who was there to be cool for anyway, in my very own living room? What I loved about smoking, after my first day as a smoker, maybe even after my first puff, was that a cigarette was a thing to reach for every single time I wanted to reach for something. It was a permanent answer to the persistent question *now what?* Perched awkwardly on the couch, my afternoons structureless, my brain dully cluttered— now what to do? Oh, yes—now for a cigarette! An easy answer, a familiar routine, a predictable experience.

"Smoking is terrible," my mother would tell me while smoking. "I don't want you to do it for the rest of your life."

"Okay," I'd say, lighting another.

Why did my mother smoke? None of her friends did, not anymore. They'd all taken it up in college—it was a little glamorous then, still—but once they'd started families, they'd quit, one after the next—all but her. And so she'd spent much of her life excusing herself at parties, stepping outside at intermissions, ducking into doorways, sneaking a quick one in the car, creating makeshift ashtrays. She was not ashamed. But she was certainly aware.

We had a running gin game. We were playing to ten thousand. By the beginning of March, she was up by four hundred points, but we hadn't even reached the halfway point. We knew the names and stories of everyone involved in the O. J. trial. We knew the events of the night of the murders as if we ourselves were on trial. We talked back to the television, shouted at the prosecutors, mocked the witnesses. When my father came home at six, we'd be sitting there still—throughout the trial, we essentially lived on West Coast time—and he'd pat me on the head.

"How're my girls?" he'd say, and we might answer or we might not, depending on what was happening on the television.

■■■ ■

The next day of my visit—was it only Saturday?—we watched more television. There was no O. J. He was in jail, knee-deep in revisionist history, but luckily for my mother and me, there was no shortage of horrendous murders committed by non-celebrities, and the news networks were happy to share: a suburban mother who'd murdered her teenage sons because she'd had enough of their smart mouths; a high school English teacher who'd murdered the basketball coach because they were both in love with the same student; a man on his honeymoon who'd killed his wife, stuffed her into a large suitcase, rolled her through JFK, and was discovered when the bag went through X-ray and her bones lit up like candles on the computer screen.

"Kevin says we love bad news," I said. "I try to explain it to him."

She rolled her eyes. "If you have to explain, it's already too late—they'll never understand."

"Exactly." I peeled open a new pack of cigarettes. It was exciting, a new pack, the promise of so many cigarettes waiting to be smoked, like a ten-day forecast with a line of sunshines. I lit the first and inhaled the smoke into every single empty space in my chest. Forget yoga—there was no better, deeper breath than this.

"Imagine being the man who sees those bones," my mother said. "Imagine unzipping that suitcase." She shuddered, but she was smiling.

"Mom," I said, exhaling what little smoke had chosen not to stay behind. "You were right about that Jason Doyle. He was horrible."

"Who?"

"Jason Doyle. The summer before senior year."

She lit her cigarette. "The one who smelled?"

"That was just the tip of the iceberg," I said.

"Well," she said. "Sometimes we—"

"And that night senior year I wasn't at Jen's house. I went to a party out in West County, and I ended up in a car with four guys I didn't even know, and for a few minutes I thought they might rape me or kill me."

She took a drag and blew it out theatrically. "You don't have to tell me everything," she said. "A mother doesn't need to know everything."

"And I almost got expelled in college for public drunkenness. If I hadn't known someone on—"

"All right," she said. "I get it. There are *secrets.*"

"I want you to know who I am," I said. "I know it sounds stupid, but I've made a lot of mistakes."

"And I've made none," she said. "Oh, thank god. Not a single one."

"Mom, seriously, I want you to know. Before it's too late."

"I do know who you are," she said. "I know you're a good parent. I know you work hard. I know you care about people. That's plenty, Christine."

I scoffed. "That's practically *nothing*. I mean, in terms of knowing someone, your own daughter."

"I don't need to know every stupid thing you've ever done. Some mistakes it's fine to keep to yourself."

"But I—"

She held up her cigarette and I stopped talking.

"You shouldn't unburden yourself entirely," she said. "Keep some burdens, or you won't have any company when I'm gone."

■■■ ■

The accident was in early February. The second week of April, after eight weeks at home, I was given the okay to return to school. The doctor smiled when he told me, then waited for me to smile, too. I did not smile. Instead, I looked across the room at my mother, who was smiling, but upon seeing me not smiling, stopped smiling. I did not wish to return to school. I liked my life just fine the way it was. There was some pain, but there would be some pain no matter where I spent my days. And there were still waves of fear, but the waves were fewer and farther between. When they struck me, my heart roared and my feet turned to stone—it was terrible, to be sure, but now this happened only a few times a week.

The fact was that, mostly, I just liked hanging out with my mother. I liked playing cards and smoking cigarettes and watching the news, in a kind of limbo as the world—pretty much everything

that lay between our house and the Santa Monica courthouse where
O. J. Simpson stood trial for murder—spun on without me. Things
out there seemed of little consequence; days of drama in the halls
of my high school were not my drama anymore. I had not been unhappy in high school; I had friends, and I liked most of my classes.
But now I could sleep until ten. For lunch, I could split a sub sandwich and a half bag of potato chips with my mother. After lunch, I
could play thirty hands of gin rummy beside an overflowing ashtray.
This clearly beat the hell out of Algebra II.

"She's ready to go back," I overheard my father tell my mother.
"The doctors say she's fine. It's time for her to get back to her life."

"The doctors don't know everything," my mother said. "She
doesn't want to go back."

I was standing in the bathroom with a frothy mouthful of toothpaste, and they were in the hallway right outside the door, apparently thinking I'd already gone to bed.

"I wouldn't want to go back either," my father said.

"Do you think I should make things unpleasant for her here?"

"You know that's not what I'm saying," my father said. "I just
think you two are having an awfully good time together. She's not
recuperating anymore. She's on vacation."

I'd held the toothpaste in my mouth so long that I was nearly
gagging on it, but I was determined to stay quiet, so I let it dribble
out of my mouth and into the sink.

"The doctor said the sooner she gets back into the swing of
things, the happier she'll be. Her life is out there waiting for her."

"Then her life can wait a little longer," my mother said. "A mother
knows. Don't look at me like I'm a fool. She had a terrible accident.
She was. She nearly. She could have—"

166

"I know," he said.

"I know," he said.

"I know," he said.

"Margie, I know," he said.

∎∎∎ ∎

On Sunday—was it Sunday? The house was so fogged with smoke that it was hard to read the calendar—we played gin. My eyes stung as I looked at the cards; our cigarettes sat smoking themselves in ashtrays as we lay down our hands and added up points. She asked me about my job. I worked for the state, making public buildings more accessible for the disabled. It was important work. People depended on me. She gave me some advice on a number of personnel situations she knew nothing about, and it was all spot-on. It was like she knew the answers to my problems before I could even get out the questions.

That night, the night before I left, I went into her room. She was lying in bed reading a magazine, and I sat on the side of her bed. When I was a child, sometimes I would come in there in the middle of the night, jolted from a frightening dream, and my father would trade beds with me, slumping down the hall to my room so I could have the safe space beside my mother. She lay the magazine down on her chest. She looked skinny in her nightgown.

"What?" she said.

"I'm sorry I don't call more often," I said.

"Oh my god," she said. "Really?"

I ignored her and went on. "I get busy, and it's just a whirlwind, and suddenly it's been two weeks and I haven't talked to you."

She set her hand on my hand. We were not touchy people. I

could count the number of times she'd hugged me. "I understand what's happening," she said. "But you don't have to do this."

"I know. But I want to. I want you to know that I think about you every day, even when I don't call."

"I appreciate that," she said. "But it's not like your father and I sit in this house all day waiting for our children to call. We do things, you know. We have lives."

"I know," I said. But secretly I did not believe her. I could not imagine having a life of my own once my children were grown. I *would* wait by the phone. I would drive them crazy. They were nine and five, and I couldn't conceive of a world when they would not be on my mind every second of every day. Was I pathetic?

"You're not pathetic," my mother said.

■■■ ■

Against the wishes of my doctors, my teachers, my father, and just about anyone else who cared to weigh in, I skipped the rest of sophomore year. I did the work. My mother even hired a tutor to get me through French. But I didn't go back to school. I stayed home, and the weather turned warm, and sometimes we sat on the front porch and smoked, and sometimes we went for short walks around the block, and no one hit me with a car. O. J. Simpson's glove didn't fit, my friends started coming over more, and my mother and I played fewer hands of gin. My friends, because they really were my friends, told me I reeked of smoke and that unless I wanted to join the burnouts in the smoking section (a small corner of the playground—the end of the era when this was allowed), I probably shouldn't bring my nasty little habit back to high school with me. And so in August I quit the cigarettes. And my mother dropped me in front of the high school on the first day of my junior year and went home alone. And when O. J. Simpson was acquitted, I was sitting in European History and didn't even know it.

■■■ ■

I woke up gasping in the middle of the night, certain that something—a large appliance, possibly—was resting on my chest. I lay in bed listening to the familiar sounds of my parents' house, indulging in a bizarre fantasy in which my lungs were dirty carpets that I could hang on the clothesline in the backyard and beat clean with a rolling pin. I went into the kitchen for some cold water.

She was sitting at the kitchen table. Her face was pinched as if she were in pain. The pack of cigarettes was beside her, but she wasn't smoking.

"Can I get you anything?" I asked.

"Check the fridge," she said. "See if there are a couple more years in there."

"Mom," I said. "One more thing. And then I promise that's it."

She looked at me with slightly squinted eyes. Maybe it wasn't pain, I thought. Maybe it was just the light. "Did you kill someone?"

"No," I said.

"Treason?"

"Seriously, okay? For one second? I just wanted to thank you."

"All right," she said. She closed her eyes. She set her fingers lightly on the pack of cigarettes but did not take one. It was as if she just wanted to assure herself they were there.

"Don't you want to know what I'm thanking you for, specifically?"

"For scraping peanut butter off your jelly sandwiches."

"For not making me go back to school that year. For letting me stay home. Everybody said it was the wrong thing to do, but somehow you knew it was right."

She opened her eyes. She took out a cigarette. "I didn't know anything," she said. She turned the cigarette in her hand, but she didn't light it. "For all I knew, I was doing terrible damage to you, *enabling* you. For all I knew, you'd live at home for the rest of your life and never do anything, never make anything of yourself. I just made it up as I went along."

"And look where I am now," I said. "All because of that. All because I knew that no matter what happened to me, I could always come home, and you would always let me stay as long as I needed to stay."

"We lucked out," she said. "We're a lucky lot, all of us."

"No," I said. "It wasn't luck, Mom. It was you."

"Stop," she said. "It's late. You've got to fly tomorrow."

"Mom—" I tried to take a deep breath, but my lungs were tight, so suddenly tight that I thought: I can never, ever smoke another cigarette again. "I won't stop," I said. "Are you listening to me? I want you to hear this. Are you listening? It was *you*."

■■■ ■

That is what I always planned to say, what I should have said, what I would have said, if the phone call that day, that suffocating July day, the day I stood in my kitchen and watched my glistening son wrap my sparkling daughter in the badminton net, had been from my mother. But it was instead from my father, his voice calm, gentle, because I was his baby girl, and it was his job to tell me this terrible thing. Your mom collapsed, he told me. In the morning. In the kitchen. Pouring herself a cup of coffee. They'd rushed her to the hospital, but there was nothing anyone could do. She had a tumor in her brain—who knew how long it had been there? Six, eight months?—and she died in the ER.

"Did she say anything?" I asked him.

"Sweetheart," he said. "There was no time."

This was unacceptable. So I tell myself the story. I *make* time. I rewrite it in my head as summer turns to fall, rewrite as I drive the children to school, as I sit at my desk at work, as I lie awake in bed long after Kevin has fallen asleep. The story's not perfect by any means. In every version, my mother gets her cigarettes back, but I alter the order of things, meddle with the point of view, change the setting. It is, and always will be, a work in progress. I indulge myself in my revisions. Sometimes my father has a larger role; other times my brothers arrive with their own bags of conflict; other times my children show up and, being children, save us all from our sadness. And sometimes my mother is angrier, and sometimes she is sicker, and sometimes she is more heroic. In one version, she and I take a train across Canada. We sit in the smoking car. We play cards on the table between our seats. We steady our trembling coffees. We nap, using our sweaters as pillows. We wake and marvel at the snow, and learn our lessons this way.

TREASURE

The truth is, I never saw the plane.

It was just after nine in the morning and we were in the S forma-
tion across the middle of the football field when, on the first note of
"Seventy-six Trombones," the unmistakable *squack* exploded from
my clarinet. Split reed. Nothing to do but make the long walk back
to the field house and get a new one from my case. I swore, broke
ranks, trudged toward the squat building that sat fifty yards behind
the end zone. I was sweaty and thirsty by the time I reached it—it
was September, still summer, really—and I gathered my hair in one
hand and bent down for a quick slurp from the drinking fountain. It
was one of those awful fountains, the kind where the water trickles
feebly from the hole, and I had to touch my lips to the spout to get a
half-decent mouthful.

I heard it then, heard it while thinking about all the lips and
tongues that had touched this fountain before mine. I heard the roar
and turned my head without lifting my mouth from the cool metal.
I did not see the plane. I saw, instead, the thirty-two-minus-one

members of the Somerville Senior High marching band lift their eyes to the sky, gaze together as with one astonished face at something I could not see, would never see (though I would say I had, and not even the people who marched beside me would remember otherwise), the friends of my youth in the shape of an S, some with instruments still at their mouths, frozen in what would surely be the most historically significant moment of their lives, they all a part now of the unfolding future, linked forever with those on the plane simply by being the last to see them—or perhaps even be seen *by* them, a giant S with one slice missing?—as they fell.

We spent three hours in lockdown, the entire student body, nearly three hundred teenagers bolted inside our redbrick and mortar, dropped only these pathetic morsels of information from the loudspeakers: there had been a plane crash; no one from the school was hurt; we would be notified with further information as it became available. But there was more, much more, that the loudspeakers were not letting on. There had to be, because why would a plane crash force the school into lockdown? And what further information could possibly become available? By midmorning rumors were swirling; the general consensus was that the plane had been carrying lethal chemicals and that the town had been poisoned, that our families were dying in their homes and cars and offices and it was only a matter of time before the toxic gasses slithered into our classrooms. By noon half the kids in school were in tears—some blubbered openly, but most cried only the misting, bewildered tears that crept back even as we blinked them away. *There has been a plane crash. No one from the school is hurt. You will be notified with further information as it becomes available.* Later we learned that some boys tried to escape out a basement window, that a distraught

174

girl had kicked out the glass door of the principal's office, that one teacher pushed another. The complex system of high school social hierarchy collapsed into a chaotic heap of cliques and types; we were at once unified in panic but each isolated in our own unique dread. No one knew how to behave. We got lost in hallways we'd traveled for four years, forgot our locker combinations, looked searchingly into the faces of unfamiliar friends.

And then, just as it seemed we were about to lose our grip, forever, on the world we knew, our parents arrived. In truth they had been arriving all morning, but they were not allowed onto the school grounds until now, and so as we looked out the windows it seemed as if they arrived en masse, a sea of quivering lips and frantic eyes rushing up the grassy slope to the school. Moments later the front doors burst outward and two hundred and eighty children, momentarily unashamed, collapsed into the arms of mothers and fathers. It was only then we learned what had really happened. For some time we stood in dumbfounded groups around the parking lot. We stood listening to car radios with family and friends until our parents, perhaps only now truly realizing the frailty of the tether that kept us all anchored to earth, took us home.

■■■　■

"Was it on fire?" Toby Hartsock asked me.

I pulled my eyes off Dean—he was mowing the lawn—and turned from the window. "Huh?"

"The plane. Did you see flames and stuff?"

"No," I said. "Nothing like that."

I turned back to watch Dean complete his final circuit, the rows in his wake as impeccable as lap lanes in a pool. I was supposed to be watching Toby, babysitting while the Hartsocks and my parents went for their weekly dinner at Ponderosa, but of late it was the elder son who held the majority of my attention. Dean liked to mow the lawn in only his swimming trunks. He didn't even wear shoes. *Living on the edge*, he'd said when I asked him if he wasn't worried about losing a toe. And he'd winked. He winked all the time now, conspiratorially, at everyone. My mother said he was turning into quite a charmer, and it was clear from her tone that she didn't mean this as a compliment.

"I'd 'a kicked sombody's ass up there," Toby said. "I never would'a let 'em crash it."

"Toby . . ." I said. But then I didn't know where to go with it. He was ten years old. What could you say? "Don't you have homework to do?"

"Did my mom leave dinner?"

"We're getting a pizza."

"Is Dean eating with us?"

"I don't know," I said. "I'm not babysitting Dean. Go do your homework and we'll order the pizza when you're done."

"You're very inflexible today," he said, on his way up the stairs. A moment later I heard Dean come into the kitchen and open the refrigerator. He was singing a song to himself. I stepped into the doorway in time to watch a bead of sweat swim down his freckled back to the waistband of his trunks. He was drinking a glass of juice and, with his free hand, picking splinters of grass from his dark brown hair. After a minute he turned.

"S'up, Kit-Kat? You sittin'?"

"Yep." I blinked. When I needed to, I could blink this Dean away and see the Dean from before, the one who once rubbed his ear wax on my paper cut to seal it.

"Cool," he said. "You guys getting pizza or what?"

"Yeah, I guess. You want some?"

"Yeah"—(and here a stumble in my heart)—"but I can't. Going out." He looked at the clock over the stove. "Shit, I'm late already. I gotta grab a shower."

And then he was gone. I rinsed out his juice glass and put it in the dishwasher, then took it out again, washed it carefully by hand, and returned it to the cupboard. I heard the *thrum* of water hitting the tub upstairs. He was up there, I thought, not ten feet above my head, eyes closed, humming a tune, naked in a hot rain.

■■■ ■

The Hartsocks had moved in next door to us when Dean and I were in the second grade. Our houses sat at the end of a dead-end street, and since we were in the same grade and walked to school together, since we each liked knock-knock jokes and KFC, since we both loved to sit in trees or under porches and pretend (sometimes for entire afternoons) to be people other than Deano and Kit-Kat, we became fast friends and remained so until middle school.

If life really can be compared to a hand of cards, I'm fairly certain that those cards remain facedown until sixth or seventh grade and only then do you get to turn them over and see who you actually are. Problem is you've already spent several years guessing what those cards are going to be, betting on your gut instincts, so when you flip the cards and discover that you don't have the hand you imagined—or that you and the person you thought you had everything in common with have very, very different cards—you have little recourse.

So it was with Dean and me. We never planned on not being friends, never intended to go in different directions, never even realized we *were* going in different directions until we'd already gone, but by the time we were thirteen we ran in different circles and had little to say to each other. We were still friendly—we often walked home from school together, and spoke superficially of teachers and kids in our grade—but instead of having after-school snacks at each other's houses in front of the TV, we amicably parted ways at the foot of his lawn.

By high school we were firmly entrenched in our separate worlds: I was band; Dean was basketball. I was newspaper; Dean was yearbook. I ran with a crowd of bright kids who made up for their anxiety by being clever, by mocking everyone who was more popular and ignoring everyone who was less popular. Dean ran with the prettier people, not the idiot jocks but the all-around guys, the ones most likely to succeed at something, certainly, because it seemed there was little they could not do. They could shoot baskets *and* maintain a B+ average. They could take pictures for the yearbook *and* get trashed on the weekends. They could be pals with the girl next door *and* date the most popular girl. Or girls. Lots of them: Rachel Cook, Celie Jenkins, Diana Wollkind, Abby Reed. I could list them chronologically, alphabetically, by height, weight, depth, IQ. I could easily list them in order of who deserved him least.

It had come as a shock to me, the sweaty palms, the thick tongue, the jelly knees. It washed over me during April of junior year, a gradual but steady wave of longing that, on the day I finally acknowledged it, named it for what it was, seized possession of me with a grip so ferocious I lost five pounds in one week and twice swooned to the floor of my front hall after brief exchanges with him in the yard. I was casually dating someone else, a boy from band, but after two weeks of loving Dean I had to break up with my trombonist. I needed to be free to pine without guilt, and once free I pined unabashedly from my bedroom window, from bio class, from the strappy lounge chair on our back deck. I pined in the shower, at my locker, over dinner, through assemblies. I gaped at couples kissing on TV, read sex articles in magazines I'd once sneered at, imagined his hands (hands I'd known when they were hairless, hands I'd reached for climbing trees) sliding up the back of my shirt.

"Pepperoni and onion!" Toby called from the top of the stairs.

I dialed the pizza place. It would be an hour, the guy said, before our pizza was delivered. Everything in town was crowded now. Whoever thought, in Somerville, you'd have to wait in line just to pump your gas?

■■■　■

Psychologists roamed the halls of the high school throughout the day. Walking counselors, they were called, the idea being that if you were uncomfortable sharing your night terrors in private you might be willing to stand in a crowded hallway and, over the din of slamming lockers, shout to a complete stranger that you couldn't get the smell of dead people out of your nose.

Special sessions were set up for "high risk groups." I was in the We Saw The Plane group with the rest of the marching band and a freshman gym class that had been playing hockey in the west parking lot.

"It sounded like somebody screaming."

"It sounded like a train."

"It sounded like a tornado."

"You ever heard a tornado?"

"No. But I know how one sounds."

"It sounded like a fucking plane crashing, you guys."

"It was trailing fire."

"Smoke."

"Sparks. Like fireworks."

"The tail fell off."

(Sometimes, though I knew this was impossible, I convinced myself that I had seen the reflection of the plane in the instruments, that the bells of the tubas had flashed to me, in an instant, the extraordinary sight.)

"The wing was hanging off."

"It had already split in two."

"It was upside down."

"Okay," the group leader said. He was no one we knew. He was a specialist, they said, when they introduced him. He specialized in things like this. What other thing was *like this*? I wondered. "That's what you saw and heard," he said. "Now tell me what you feel about it."

Silence. Not even a rustle, for probably a full minute. Finally somebody sneezed.

The thing was, really, the thing no one would dare say, is that we were secretly thrilled that something had happened in our sleepy lives, that whatever residual terror seized us in our most vulnerable moments was outweighed by the pride and excitement of seeing four hundred news vans lining the eight dilapidated blocks that was downtown Somerville. It was not that we were happy it had happened; we were simply happy that, if it had to happen somewhere, it had happened *here*.

■■■ ■

"Caroline Gable found half a shoe in their backyard yesterday," my mother said over dinner. "They're almost two miles from where it went down."

"Christ," my father said, setting down his fork. "Not at the table. Let there be one place—"

"We should look on the roof," my mother said. "We should make sure there's nothing there."

"I'll climb up tomorrow," my father said. He looked at me wearily.

"How ya doin'?"

"I'm all right," I said.

"Sure?"

"Sure," I said. "I'm busy. We're doing a special issue of the paper."

"When I was a senior in high school," he said, "we did a special issue of the paper when our quiz bowl team won at state." He traced the lip of his water glass with his index finger. "I can't even—" He stopped. Even *what*? he must have been thinking. He did not know. All he knew was that tomorrow he had to climb onto the roof of his home to look for pieces of shoes.

"It's okay, Dad," I said. "We're all okay."

"Listen to her," my mother said. "Everyone's okay."

My father put his head in his hands. "Jesus Christ," he said. "Those people."

"Tell him again, Katie," my mother said.

■■■ ■

That was September, of course. By mid-October all the roofs in Somerville had been checked. The news vans had migrated north to the turnpike and then scattered in the numerous directions of new threats. Only a few strangers remained in Somerville—counselors, investigators, coroners—and they, too, were beginning to pack away their bags of tricks. You could look around town and see that it was the same as it had been in August, the same barbershop and diner, the same cracked sidewalks and battered stop signs. It could seem like a dream. And like a dream, it slowly sank from view. Like a dream, it descended from the sky and took root under our feet until instead of it being something we had to squint to see it became the very ground we walked on.

"You know there's treasure in the woods," Toby Hartsock told me one Sunday evening as I prepared to shut off the light in his bedroom.

I paused at the switch. "What are you talking about?"

"Gold," he said. "And diamonds. Rings and watches and stuff that fell out of the plane. It's spread all over the woods."

"Toby," I said. "That's crazy."

He scrambled out of bed. "Check this out." He opened the top drawer of his dresser and took out a tube sock that was spooled into a ball, unwound it and reached in, then removed his hand. He unfolded his small fist in front of me; inside was a tiny gold stud. "I found it in the woods behind the Burger King. That's less than a mile from where it went down. It could be worth like a hundred bucks or something."

"Toby, some girl probably lost that. It's probably from Walmart."

He scowled. "Nuh-uh. Why would a girl be in the woods behind the Burger King?"

Well, what could I say? In another few years he'd know why a girl would be in the woods behind the Burger King. He'd know about the places high school kids went—not me, not my crowd, but lots of others, including Dean, I was sure—to drink beer, to pass a joint around a sloppy campfire, to hook up under cover of the thick, towering trees.

"What were you doing back there anyway?" I asked him.

He sat down cross-legged on his bed. "Adam Lefton and me were at Burger King. He started telling me about all this stuff you could find in the woods and so we went looking. I found this in like a half hour." He closed his fist around the stud. "It's not just us. Lots of kids are doing it."

"But Toby," I said, "right after, the FBI and all those guys, they combed the woods. If anything was left—"

"They didn't look everywhere," he said. He got under the covers, the stud still in his grasp. "I'll bet ya they didn't get down in the brush. Or those skanky ponds. Plus they were just looking for evidence. We're looking for treasure."

I shut out the light. "Whatever you say, Tobes."

Downstairs, on the Hartsocks' couch, I set about pretending to do my homework. I was trying to get through *The Tempest* for AP English, but trying to get through *anything* while sitting in the Hartsocks' living room was next to impossible. The babysitting job was a total ruse—I'd pretty much given up sitting at fifteen—but in the last six months was always available for Mrs. Hartsock, day or night, weekday or weekend. Last minute? No problem! Sitting for Toby had become an excuse to sit among the things Dean touched every day, to imagine myself in this house not as a babysitter but a girlfriend. I'd sit on their overstuffed sofa with a book in my lap and consciously detach myself from reality, pretending he'd just gotten up from beside me, was in the kitchen fixing something for us to eat. Sometimes I'd look over my shoulder impatiently, wondering what was taking him so long. On more than one occasion I'd become so lost in the fantasy that I'd nearly called out his name to hurry him along.

"Katie?"

It took me a moment to realize he was actually there, standing in the kitchen doorway. He was wearing sweats and his Somerville Basketball T-shirt and his hair was wet and slicked back and he was just standing there smiling at me.

"Hey," I said, wrenching myself from the dream. I could almost hear the ripping noise. "Hey. What's up?"

"You looked really freaky just then," he said.

"Thanks."

"No, I mean. You just . . . what're you thinking about?"

"Nothing," I said. "I mean, you know." I held up the book cheerfully. "Shakespeare or something."

He came and sat on the couch beside me. I inched myself away so that if one of us shifted, our knees would not accidentally touch. He smelled like honey shampoo and I either wanted to bury my nose in his brown hair or vomit on my shoes. There seemed to be no other choice.

"You know what I was thinking just now, watching you?"

I swallowed what felt like a walnut. "What?"

He grinned. His top front teeth were a tiny bit gapped and crooked, a flaw that would have made most guys unappealing but somehow worked to his advantage. It was this imperfect thing that made his face perfect. "We used to do some crazy stuff, you and me. We were really whacked out."

"Yeah," I said.

"Remember that time you put on my clothes and I put on your clothes and we thought we could fool people into thinking you were me and I was you?" He snorted a laugh. "Who does that?"

"We were really stupid," I said. "And we were like eight then. I can't believe we thought that would work."

"It's different now, with kids," he said. I saw his eyes pass over Toby's picture on the mantel. "They start worrying about being cool when they're in kindergarten. They'd never be crazy like we were. It makes me feel really old, you know?"

"We are old," I said. "We're seniors."

"Whoever thought we'd be so old?" he said. He paused and his face turned serious. "I been thinking about you," he said. "A lot."

I tried to look casually intrigued. "Oh yeah?"

"You know why?"

My voice wouldn't come so I shook my head.

He sat forward, put his elbows on his knees and his chin in his hands, looked at the floor. "'Cause you saw the plane," he said. He glanced over at me. "I know this sounds crazy but I'm kinda jealous. I mean, I know it was really horrible for you guys, and I feel bad for saying it—"

"Don't feel bad," I said.

"I just mean, you know . . ." He looked straight at me. "Were you scared?"

For a moment I thought maybe I could tell him, my friend Dean. Yes, I could tell him. I could say, listen, here's a funny thing: my reed was broken, and then I stopped for a drink of water. But he was sitting beside me, the shift of his weight tilting us closer on the couch, and for the first time in a long time what I said mattered to him.

"Yeah," I said. "Sure. I thought . . . I thought maybe . . . you know . . . it was like it wasn't real, like I was seeing myself see it, but . . . yeah, it was, I was. Yeah. You know?"

He shook his head. "I just wish I had a little piece of it, Katie," he said. "You have your piece. You saw it. So it's like you're *my* little piece of it now." He smiled cautiously. "That's weird, isn't it? I mean, I know it is. It's weird."

"It's not weird," I said.

"Well, I guess maybe it's not any weirder than anything else right now."

"I love you," I said. But by the time I said this it was four hours later and I was lying in my bed next door, talking to the empty space beside me that for almost six months now had been named Dean.

"I've been waiting so long to hear you say that," the empty space said.

"The wait's over," I said. "We don't have to wait for anything anymore."

I turned over and looked at the clock. It was almost 2:00 a.m. I got out of bed and went downstairs, thinking a cup of tea might settle my thoughts and let me get some sleep. I found my mother sitting at the kitchen table eating cheese and crackers and reading an admissions brochure from the University of Pittsburgh.

"What're you doing?" I asked.

She glanced up. Her narrow reading glasses were perched on the tip of her nose and she had a pencil behind her ear. "Did you know every room at Pitt has its own microwave? Isn't that clever?"

"Lots of places do that now," I said, pulling a mug from the cupboard. "And Pitt's out, remember?"

"I was just . . . revisiting," she said. "You know they have one of the top ranked fitness centers in the country?"

"You want me to pick a school because they have great treadmills?" I sat down while my water heated in the teakettle. "What are you doing awake?"

She pushed up her glasses. "I was hungry. I wanted some cheese."

"I didn't like Pitt," I said.

"But you could come home on weekends," she said. "I could do your laundry for you. You'd be the envy of all your friends."

I smirked. "Actually, no, they'd feel sorry for me."

She took the pencil from her ear and laid it on the table beside the brochure. "You don't have to be nasty about it."

"I'm not. I'm kidding, okay? It's just . . . I have my list. I feel good about it."

"Katie, honey," she said. Then she whispered: "Do you know how much your father wants you to live close to home?"

My mother blamed a lot on my father—the leaky pipes, the sullen cat, the patch of grass that never turned green—but this was a new one, so desperate she was not to blow her cover.

"Tell him I'll be fine," I said. "Tell him I'm not going to the other side of the world."

"Every time you walk out of this house it's the other side of the world." She sliced a piece of cheese and placed it on her cracker. "As far as he's concerned."

■■■ ■

The Saturday before Halloween Mrs. Hartsock called and asked me to babysit for Toby. They'd gotten last-minute tickets to a hockey game in Pittsburgh and would not be back until after midnight. Toby was going to a fifth grade costume party down the block, but had been instructed to be home by 9:00. Dean, I knew from other sources, was going to a Halloween party thrown by the basketball team, so I would be free to pine among his things in peace.

I was watching TV when Toby arrived home. He was dressed as a hobo—a torn coat three sizes too big, a tattered engineer's hat, a stick over his shoulder with a bandanna-bag attached. He had three friends in tow: a skeleton, a ninja, and a boxer, who all grunted as they passed.

"We're gonna play Xbox in the basement," Toby said.

"Sure," I said. I didn't care when he went to bed, as long as it was sometime before his parents returned. I heard them down there, those boys, playing their games. I thought of Dean and me, how we would someday tell our children how we'd met so young, been best friends, then a little later more than friends, how we would skip over the middle part, these last few years, because that would no longer be an interesting or relevant part of the story, and the further we got from it the more this time we'd spent apart would shrink to nothing until it would seem there had only been a day, perhaps an hour, between the time we drifted apart and the time we came back together.

I fell asleep. When I woke the clock above the TV said 11:30 and the house was quiet. I went to the top of the basement steps. The lights were still on but everything was silent; no way there were four boys, even two, even one, down there. I took the stairs to the second floor two at a time, holding out a tiny glimmer of hope that Toby'd seen me asleep on the couch and gone to bed of his own accord. Of course this was not the case; his room was empty.

"Shit," I said.

Then, from downstairs, came the sound of the front door closing. Quietly. I had never yelled at Toby before, never had reason to, but now he was in for it. What if the Hartsocks had come home early and found me asleep on the couch and him gone, at 11:00 on a Saturday night? I stormed down the stairs and came upon Dean, standing at the mirror in the front hall, wiping white paint from his cheeks with a paper napkin.

"S'up, Kit-Kat?" he asked, his reflection acknowledging me with a nod. He was dressed as some garden variety ghoul: tight black pants, black turtleneck, white face, lips thick with bloody lipstick.

"Nothing," I said.

"I scare you?" He burped, then smiled. "You don't look so hot. You look like, I dunno, like maybe—"

"I'm fine," I said. He smelled as if he'd swum in the keg before pumping it. He went to work on his nose; the paint fell in flakes on the tiled hall floor.

"Tobes asleep?"

"No," I said, before it occurred to me to lie, to cover my own ass.

"No?" He turned. His forehead and chin were still white, his lips still red. Only his cheeks and nose were the color of flesh, and somehow this looked ever more ghoulish, half dead and half alive.

"I don't know where he is," I said. "He was downstairs playing Xbox with his friends and now he's gone."

"You didn't hear 'em go out?"

"No. I—I must have been in the bathroom or something."

"That little shit. Time are my parents coming home?"

"I don't know. Like, in an hour or something."

"Moron," he said. "What's he thinking? Where would a bunch of ten-year-olds go at this hour?"

I drove his car to the Burger King parking lot; though he'd driven home from the party, I thought it best to designate myself his driver for the rest of the evening. The car stank of beer and (I was almost certain) Rachel Cook's perfume. Where'd she gone? I wondered. And why had he come home so early? I snuck a look over at him as I drove. His eyes were closed. He had his fingers hooked in the collar of his turtleneck, pulled away from his throat as if he were having trouble breathing. Perhaps they'd broken up.

"Dean," I said gently. "We're here. But I can go look for them myself. You don't have to—"

"I'm okay," he said, sitting up straight. "I'm good. I just needed a little down time."

The night was cold and the ground squished under our feet as we made our way into the woods. In another few days the frost would come and the ground would get hard and the scorched earth where the wreckage had smoldered would turn brittle.

"This sucks," Dean said. He stumbled over a root and had to do a little dance to keep upright.

"We should have brought a flashlight," I said. "You have one in your car?"

"Nah. I'm an idiot, Katie. I never have anything I need. Never. I swear, I'm like—"

"Drunk," I said. "You're drunk. You're not an idiot."

"Why'd we stop bein' friends?" Dean asked.

"We're still friends," I said. Something scuttled under a nearby branch; the moon slid out from a cloud and illuminated the tops of the trees.

"You know what I mean. You were my best friend, Kit-Kat . . . Katie. You stood out there and watched that plane. You've always been there. You're the best girl I've ever known. You're the best—"

"Dean," I said. "Shut up, okay? You're really drunk."

"So? That doesn't mean it's not true."

He grabbed my wrist. Maybe if it had been my hand he'd grabbed I would have felt differently about the whole thing. Maybe it would have been sweet and clumsy and endearing. Not that he knew either way; he'd just grabbed, and come up with what he came up with.

"You're awesome, Katie," he said.

He yanked me roughly back toward him and kissed me hard. His lips were tacky with lipstick and the thick taste of beer in his mouth made me gag. His grip on my wrist tightened and he locked his other arm across the small of my back and thrust himself against me. I felt as panicked as if I'd been jumped by a complete stranger, a faceless man who'd leapt from behind a tree. I forced myself to think *I am kissing Dean I am kissing Dean* and for a moment I let myself into it, thinking that it didn't matter why Dean was kissing me and it didn't matter where we were or anything but this kiss and his arms around me and as I gave into him in that instant I felt my knees give and then we toppled onto the wet ground. And he was on top of me and he was heavy, so heavy, and all I could think was how could I not have thought about how heavy a person would be on top of me? How in all my times imagining this, every detail and sensation, could I have neglected to consider the sheer weight of a man? Other things—the stink of his breath, his fingernails digging in my wrist, his flaking white forehead, the twigs stabbing my back, the cold, damp leaves mashing up under the collar of my shirt— none of these things in the moment were more of a surprise than the physical burden of being under Dean.

I might have told him some of this, were I not being suffocated, but all I could muster was "Dean . . ." and even that was said so softly that I myself almost mistook it for a coo of passion. "Dean . . ." I tried again. "Dean, stop."

He paused and raised his head, his eyes wide, his bloody lips parted.

"You hear that?" he asked.

"It was me," I said, my voice trembling. "I—"

"No," he said. He spun off me and in one move was upright. "It was them."

For a moment I'd forgotten why we were out here. "What? Who?"

"The kids," he said. "Listen . . ."

Instead of listening, I took the opportunity to sit up, to wipe the muck from my back. And then, as I struggled to my knees, my heart still racing and my breath still short, I heard a whoop from the distance.

"That's Toby," Dean said. "That goddamn—"

He took a few steps away from me, in the direction of the sound, then stopped and turned back. I was still on my knees in the mud. His face softened.

"Shit, Katie," he said. He put his hand down to me and I took it and let him pull me to my feet. His hand was coarse and cold, and as we walked a few steps deeper into the woods I let my fingers slip from his.

"Jesus," he said. "That was stupid back there. I don't know what I was thinking."

"Whatever," I said. I didn't even know what he thought was stupid: kissing me, or kissing me the way he did. "It doesn't matter."

"I'm sorta drunk," he said. "You know how sometimes you just want to know how it would be with a person? You know, somebody you've known forever? I guess that's kinda stupid."

"I guess," I said.

"I didn't—" he started. "I mean, I didn't hurt you or do something or—"

"It's okay," I said. "I'm okay."

"I guess this is one of those things you look back on and it's funny," he said. "Like when we're forty or something we'll talk about the time we made out in the woods."

"Sure," I said, though I knew for certain that we would not speak of it again, ever, that not only would Dean Hartsock never be my boyfriend but that he would also never be my friend. He was my neighbor, my acquaintance by coincidence. He was the boy I played with when I was a child.

I saw their costumes first, in the light of the moon that filtered through the trees. A ninja, a skeleton, a boxer, and a hobo, cast off, crumpled in piles at the edge of the water. The four naked boys walked silent circles around the murky pond, the brown water lapping against their hairless chests. Their eyes were closed, their faces pressed in concentration. I imagined their toes clenching the mud.

"Jesus," Dean whispered. We crouched down in the brush. "What're they doing?"

"They're on a treasure hunt," I said.

"Jesus," he said again. "In that shit?" I thought then that he would yell at his brother, that—now sober, his wits about him—he would lay into all four of them, haul them out of the filthy water and march them back half-naked through the woods, raging the whole time about how he had to come out here and track them down.

"Kit-Kat," he whispered.

I turned to him. He was smiling. "What?"

"That's just like something we woulda done. I love it. It's totally crazy."

"Hey, Dean!" Toby shouted, catching sight of us. "Hey, Dean! Check this out!"

Dean stood and unzipped his pants. "You guys find anything?"

"Tyler found a bobby pin!"

He looked down at me. "What d'ya say? Let's take a look, huh?"

I just stared at him. My brain was numb, my bones humming. After a moment he stepped out of his jeans, pulled his shirt over his head. Then, nearly naked in the dark, he reached for my face and wiped my bottom lip gently with his thumb. When he took his thumb away it was bright red.

A bobby pin. Was there anything worth *less* than a bobby pin? Had anyone ever regretted the loss of one, dislodged during gym class or shopping for sweaters? The one buried in the mud in the middle of these woods could have come from a hundred different places, could have slipped from the hair of a girl on her back, before the plane, before any of this. And yet I watched them, unable in that moment to walk away from Dean, or from those boys who believed that the treasure they unearthed might bear some resemblance to the treasure they'd imagined. What exactly were they hoping to find? Something to give back to the people of our town, something we could keep as a memento, something to say, we were here, we saw it, we lived under it and now we live over it, this land, this water, we will walk in circles forever searching and some day we will find something that explains it all, something that says here is what transpired and here is why it is important. Here. Here. A gift from us. For you.

ACKNOWLEDGMENTS

Thanks to my brilliant editor and friend, Marysue Rucci, for sticking with me. I could not ask for a smarter reader, a more patient editor, or a more enthusiastic cheerleader. And thanks to the rest of the team at Simon & Schuster, especially the talented and unflappable duo of Elizabeth Breeden and Laura Regan.

Immense thanks goes to my BFF&N Mary Beth Berger Baken, who has been my most thoughtful reader and my lifelong pen pal, beginning when we lived next door to each other.

Thanks also to Randolph Thomas and Brad Barkley and Marion Winik for their consistent good advice and unwillingness to let me get away with much.

Thanks to my friends and colleagues at Dickinson College for their support, and a most enthusiastic shout-out to my amazing students, past and present, who are a constant source of information and inspiration.

Thanks to Betsy Perabo for her seemingly effortless expertise as sister and friend and reader. And to my parents who continue to inspire me as a parent and teacher and writer.

ACKNOWLEDGMENTS

Thanks and love to my amazing children for giving me the two best excuses in the world for taking fifteen years to write this book. And to Sha'an Chilson for giving me a million reasons to get up from my desk and a million reasons to go back to it. Do I know how lucky I am? I do. I do. I do.

Finally, always, thanks to my beloved teachers and classmates at the University of Arkansas, many of whose hands will never touch these pages, but whose wisdom and humanity has touched all these words.

ABOUT THE AUTHOR

Susan Perabo is Writer in Residence and Professor of English at Dickinson College in Carlisle, Pennsylvania. She is the author of a collection of short stories, *Who I Was Supposed to Be*, and a novel, *The Broken Places*. Her fiction has been anthologized in *Best American Short Stories*, *The Pushcart Prize*, and *New Stories from the South* and has appeared in numerous magazines, including *One Story*, *Glimmer Train*, *The Iowa Review*, *The Missouri Review*, and *The Sun*.